SECRET OF THE SATILFA

Secret
of the Satilfa

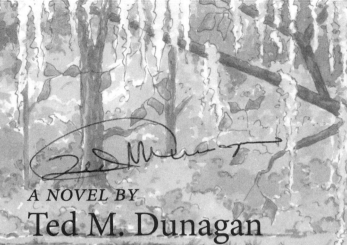

A NOVEL BY
Ted M. Dunagan

Junebug Books
Montgomery Louisville

Junebug Books
105 South Court Street
Montgomery, AL 36104

Library of Congress Cataloging-in-Publication Data
available upon request.

ISBN-13: 978-1-58838-249-8
ISBN-10: 1-58838-249-4

LCCN: 2010009523

Title page illustration and "The Setting" on pages 8–9
by Linda Aldridge.

Design by Randall Williams

Printed in the United States of America
by Sheridan Books.

TO MY BROTHERS,
NED AND FRED,
WHO WERE THERE WITH ME.

Contents

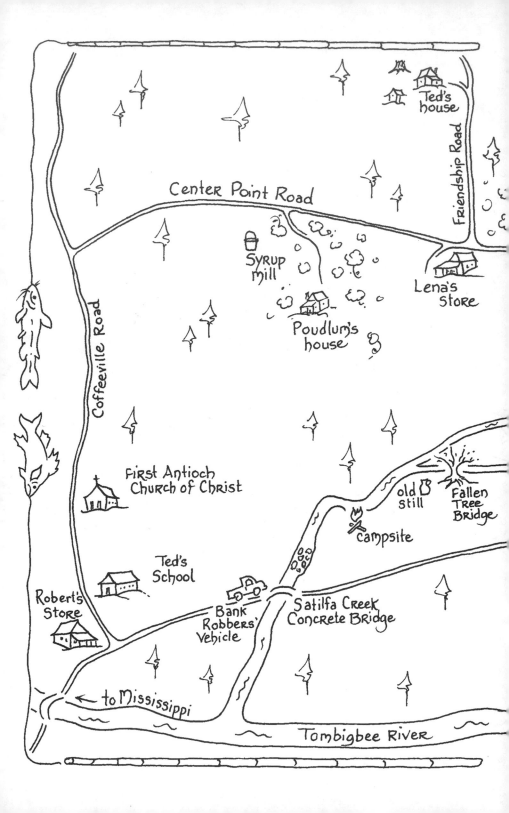

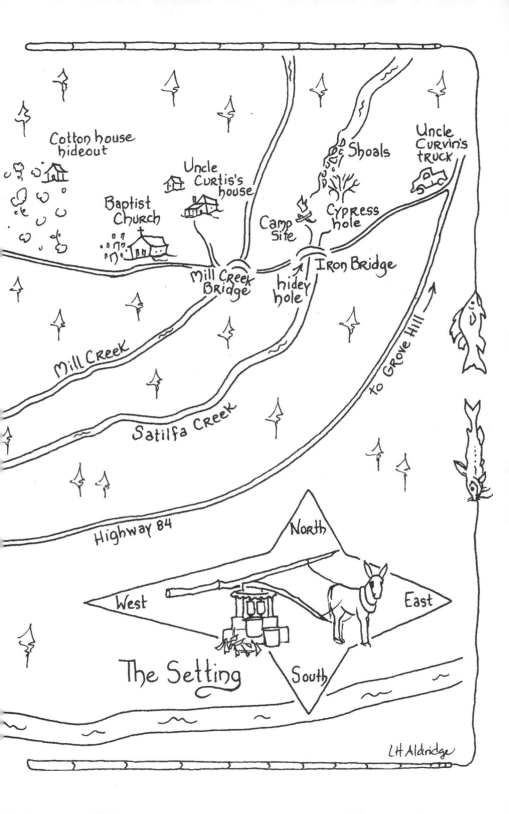

CHAPTER ONE

THE STUMP

It was just a stump now, but once it had been a grand and glorious tree that soared far above the ground with great branches that spread like a protective umbrella over its part of the world. Its thick canopy had given protection from the elements to both man and beast for a long, long time.

The very thing that killed it was the force from which it had once given protection to others. On a stormy day when the wind roared and the rain lashed, a jagged bolt of lightning raced from the clouds, struck the great tree, and shattered the life out of it all the way down to the tips of its roots deep beneath the surface of the earth.

I missed that old tree, and also the nuts the squirrels and I had collected from it. They were hard to crack and the meat inside was minuscule, but sweet and tasty. After I had cracked the nut, I used the curved end of one of my momma's hairpins to pick out the meat. It had been a black walnut tree.

After the tree had been dead for awhile, sometimes during a full moon I would gaze out the window and marvel at the amazing display of shadow and light the moonshine played upon its bare, silver branches.

Then one day my father and some other men came in a big log truck with chains, ropes, axes, and a crosscut saw, and with two mules tied behind.

The men cut the dead tree down. It crashed to the ground with a thunderous roar and its dead branches shattered and exploded into the air.

They used the mules to load that giant tree trunk on the truck. I heard one of the men say they were going to take it to a sawmill, that black walnut was very valuable wood. I wondered where they were taking the old tree. There had been a sawmill about a mile from our house, but it had closed back in the late summer.

The men cut up all the branches, and my two older brothers, Ned and Fred, stacked them to be used as firewood. That was a good thing because winter was coming and we would be burning a lot of wood soon.

I had loved that tree, but now it was gone with only its stump left like a tombstone that shone in the moonlight, to remind the world it had lived long and served a purpose in the world.

I hung out around that stump a lot, and that's where I was on Saturday afternoon when I heard Fred approaching from toward the house.

"Hey, boy, what you doing?" he called out.

"Cracking nuts," I replied.

"What kind of nuts? There ain't no more walnuts out here."

"I picked up some hickory nuts while I was squirrel hunting with Ned this morning."

"What for? There's even less meat in a hickory nut than in a black walnut. You wasting your time, unless you are a squirrel."

"Nothing better to do."

"Wanna bet?" my brother said.

I paused from digging around inside that nut with my hairpin and looked up at him. I knew my brother, and I could tell from the look on his face that something was up. He was good at making up games and building toys. We had toy log trucks and bows and arrows he had made, but we had grown tired of both. Now, he had something new he was hiding behind his back.

It was getting dark before we left the stump. We had sat around it for hours playing checkers on a checkerboard my brother had made from a piece of cardboard he had cut from the side of a box that apples had been shipped in. On the outside was a picture of a big red apple, but on the plain inside he had used his ruler and a pencil to draw off the sixty-four squares of a checkerboard, after which he had colored every other square black or red with some stubby crayons.

The checkers we used were the tops off Nehi and RC Cola drink bottles, which he had gotten out of the drink box over at Miss Lena's Store. He played with his bottle caps right side up and I turned mine upside down.

"It's your move," he told me.

"I can't hardly see anymore. I can't even tell which of my checkers has been crowned."

"All right, we'll call this game a draw," Fred said as he raked the bottle caps up and put them in his pocket. "You know, this old stump ought to be good for something besides a place to crack nuts and play checkers."

"Like what?" I asked him.

"I don't know, but I'll be thinking on it."

My stomach reminded me what time it was. "What do you think we're having for supper?"

Fred turned toward our house, leaned his head back, inhaled deeply and said, "I think it's collard greens, baked sweet potatoes, and corn bread."

"You can smell all that?" I asked in amazement.

"Well, not the cornbread, but you know we gonna have that."

It was late October in the fall of 1948, and there was a chill in the air as we walked toward the house.

"It's gonna get cold tonight," Fred said. "I'll take a load of wood in with me and start a fire in the fireplace. You grab a load of stove wood for the kitchen."

There was a large pile of stove wood beside the chopping block where our oldest brother Ned had split it. This was the wood for the kitchen stove, split into small pieces so our momma could feed them into the little door of the fire box.

I never complained, but I hated that job because every time I carried a load of stove wood toward the back door leading into the kitchen, the sharp edges of the pieces cut into my arms. It was worse in the summertime when fat green caterpillars sometimes hid on the wood and I would squish them on my arms. That really gave me the creeps.

The only thing worse was stepping in chicken droppings when I was barefoot and getting it between my toes.

As I knelt beside the woodpile and loaded my arms, I was thankful that it had gotten cool and I didn't have to worry about fuzzy or slimy caterpillars. And, I had my shoes on in case a chicken had gotten out of the pen.

Fred had been correct about what was for supper, except for one thing: he hadn't sniffed out the blackberry cobbler that was sitting on the apron of the stove.

It was all good. The collards were tasty, especially the pot likker, which I crumbled my cornbread into and ate with a spoon. The baked sweet potatoes had little droplets of moisture on the outside of the heavy skins. We peeled and put butter on them and ate them with the cornbread, and washed it all down with a big glass of sweet milk.

After all that my momma dished out the blackberry cobbler in servings large enough so nobody needed any seconds.

Everything was good, but the sweet potatoes had been my favorite. I noticed there were some raw ones lying on the counter and figured my momma planned to slice them real thin and fry them up for breakfast.

Most sweet potatoes were red or orange inside, but occasionally you would come across a white one. Folks argued about which was the best, but I really couldn't tell much difference. I just knew that we always had plenty of them. The good thing about sweet potatoes was that they would keep all winter. All you had to do was build yourself a potato bank, which was pretty simple.

Sweet potatoes were harvested in the fall after they

grew underneath the ground like roots to vines that grew above the ground. What you did was plow or dig them up sometime in October before it got real cold.

My Uncle Curvin grew them on a piece of land he sharecropped down near Coffeeville. I had helped him plant them back during the first part of July. He always said you had to get the little potato sets in the ground by July 5. He had brought us a pickup truck load last week, and we had fixed us a potato bank.

I don't know if it was called a potato bank because it was where you saved your potatoes, or because you banked dirt around them and then covered them with pine straw and more dirt. Anyway, when you wanted to bake them, fry them, or make a potato pie, you just dug through the dirt and pine straw and pulled out what you needed.

Later that evening after the fire in the fireplace had died down, we roasted some peanuts by putting them in a flat pan and setting it on some hot coals pulled out onto the hearth.

The fire made me drowsy, and it wasn't long before Momma chased us off to bed. Fred beat me into bed and told me to close the window.

Just before I closed it I gazed toward where the great tree had stood and imagined it still being there. I remembered begging my father not to cut it down, but he explained that it was dead and would eventually become a hazard by falling down on its own. Instead of letting it do that or rot, it was better to get some lumber and some firewood out of it.

He told me that I would encounter a lot of dead trees in

my life, and that I needed to learn they should be disposed of and how to accomplish that.

I figured out later that he was comparing dead trees to situations in life, and I thought that did make some sense.

The other thing he used the tree to teach me was that you could save things in your memory. "Do you remember what it used to look like?" he asked me.

"Yes, sir. It was the biggest and prettiest tree I've ever seen, and it was real easy to climb."

"Well, then," he said, "that tree will live forever in your memory, and no one or anything can kill it or cut it down."

From then on I concentrated on remembering good and pleasant things and cutting down and hauling away the bad things in my memory.

I missed my daddy. He was on an island way off in the Pacific Ocean. He was so far away that I couldn't even imagine the distance.

After the sawmill behind Miss Lena's Store over on Center Point Road closed, he was out of work for a while. He went down to Mobile and picked up some carpentry work, but that, too, had played out. I don't know how or when he found out about the civil service job on Guam Island, where they were rebuilding after World War II, but off he went, signing up for a year of service. Even though he was gone, he didn't forget about us. Every month he sent Momma a check for forty dollars, which more than bought groceries and the other needs of our family.

My daydreaming was interrupted when Fred said, "Hey, close the window and get to bed. We got to get up early tomorrow morning and go to church. They're introducing a new preacher and we'll probably be stuck in there till the cows come home."

Our last preacher had lost his position for drinking on the job. We had heard he was over in Mississippi, had himself a new church, and was dealing with his demons quite well.

I closed the window and slid between the sheets and pulled a quilt up over me. It wasn't long before my brothers began dueling like two bull frogs with their snoring.

I pulled the covers up over my head and fell into a dream world where trees were never cut down and where your daddy never had to go off to some island we had never heard of.

Some time during the night it got colder, and I pulled an extra quilt up over myself and went back to sleep wondering what the morrow would bring, other than having to go to church.

I liked the new preacher right off. When we walked through the front door of the Center Point Road Baptist Church, he grinned, tousled my hair, and gave me an assuring wink.

Once he got started preaching, I was happy to see he didn't rant and rave like the old preacher. He didn't stomp around, point fingers, yell amens, or work up to a fever pitch.

His name was Brother Earnest Hillsboro and he said he had fought over in Germany during the great war we were attempting to recover from.

I don't think he liked war too much because he talked

about it a lot while he preached and he concluded his sermon by saying, "War is always about young men fighting and dying while old men talk and plan. Perhaps one day if the young men could withstand the enticement rendered by the rhetoric and reject the call to arms, no one would die, no one would have to grieve over lost loved ones, and the horror of war would cease to be.

"However," he continued, "young men believe they are immortal and old men can't stop talking, so the wars go on while the children, the women, and the innocent suffer its consequences."

The church was so quiet you could have heard a gnat's wings buzzing.

Fred and I usually played some subtle game to pass the time in church, but when I glanced his way, I saw that he, too, was absorbed with what the new preacher was saying.

Brother Hillsboro took a deep breath and continued, "Yet when evil raises its ugly head, who can defend us better than the strong young men, and who can plan better than the wise old men who have fought and survived wars themselves when they were young men?"

Everyone in the congregation sat frozen in place waiting for the preacher to answer his own question.

"The answer eludes us. We can only hope and pray the young men stay strong and brave, and that the old men are wise and resourceful. The truth is, there is a far better King than anyone leading an earthly army. All we poor mortals can do is pray, have faith, and praise Him."

The new preacher was a big hit. After he had dismissed the service, I noticed that all the adults gathered around him outside the church, shaking his hand and telling him how much they had enjoyed his sermon.

Fred and I sat on the running board of Uncle Curvin's old pickup truck watching everyone mill around in their Sunday finest.

"I think everybody likes the new preacher," I said.

"Yeah," Fred replied. "He'll be eating free fried chicken dinners for a month of Sundays."

Uncle Curvin took us all home, and Fred disappeared shortly after that. He didn't tell me where he was going, but he said to meet him out by the stump later.

I had just about forgotten his request, but I was out at the stump digging around with my hairpin attempting to get a speck of meat out of a hickory nut when I heard the ruckus.

It wasn't like anything I had heard before either. It was coming from the thick woods toward the trail which led through them to Friendship Road, and it was a combination of sounds. At first I thought it was a wild pig because of the grunting, scraping, grinding, and rustling racket.

Little chill willies jumped up all over me, but I forced myself to venture into the edge of the woods to investigate. When I saw what it was, I just stood there, my feet frozen to the ground.

CHAPTER TWO

THE SPINNING JENNY

I t was my brother dragging a long piece of lumber through the woods, a two-by-six pine board!

"Well, don't just stand there gawking," he said. "Come help me. This thing is mighty heavy, and I got splinters in my hands from dragging it."

"Where did you get that thing?" I asked.

"Found it about half buried back behind Miss Lena's Store where the sawmill used to be."

"How long do you 'spect it is?"

"I stepped it off and it's about twenty-four feet."

"What you planning on doing with it?"

"We gonna put it on that stump and make us a spinning jenny."

"I never heard tell of such a thing. What's a spinning jenny?"

"I'll tell you later. Right now I need you to grab a holt and help me drag this thing the rest of the way to the stump"

By the time we got to the stump, I was marveling at the feat my brother had accomplished by dragging that big board all the way from where the sawmill used to be. But he was almost three years older than me, and real big and strong for his age.

"What now?" I asked.

"You pick up the other end while I pick up this end and let's lay it across the stump so the same length of board hangs off each side of it."

After we did that my brother walked a circle around the stump and the board studying it all the while.

"So what's it supposed to do?"

"Can't you see? We got to drill a hole in the very center of that board and attach it to the stump so it will spin around without it coming off."

"How we gonna do that?"

"I ain't figured that out yet. You don't do nothing but ask questions; why can't you come up with some answers?"

I thought about it for a little while and it came to me. "After we drill a hole in the center of the board, we have to drill a hole in the center of the stump, drive an iron bar or something into that hole, then just drop the board on it so the iron bar goes through the hole in the board."

"Hey! That'll work, but where we gonna get an iron bar?"

We had an old Radio Flyer wagon that we had worn the wheels off pulling it through the woods and fields hauling everything from water to watermelons. Since then it had been over in the shed just rusting away. "Why don't we take one of the axles out of that old wagon in the shed?"

"But we been planning to put new wheels on it," Fred protested.

"Yeah, we been planning to do that for two years now, and besides, we way too big to be playing with that wagon anymore."

We headed to the shed where we extracted one of the axles from the disabled wagon, took our father's auger and a large drill bit and a tape measure, and returned to the stump and the board.

After measuring and finding the exact center of the board, I held it steady while Fred drilled the hole in it.

I brushed away the curly wood slivers and said, "Now let's get to that stump."

We didn't even have to measure to find the exact center of the stump. On the inside of trees there is a perfect circle for each year of its age starting from the center and working outward. The circles were still faintly visible on the old stump. I had counted them before and knew the tree had been eighty years old when the lightning bolt killed it.

Fred placed the point of the drill bit on the dot in the exact center of the stump. I thought the tree must have been just a little bitty fellow when that dot first appeared.I watched as my brother began drilling at the spot indicating when the tree had been born.

"How long you figure that axle is?" Fred asked after he blew the wood shavings from the hole he had drilled in the stump.

I placed the tape measure on it and announced, "It's exactly two feet."

"That hole I drilled is deep enough then. It's four or five inches. We'll drive the axle down about halfway so it'll be real tight and still leave a foot sticking out of the stump to go through the board. Go get the ax off the chopping block so I can drive it in."

The flat part of the ax made a chiming sound as it drove the axle deep into the stump. Fred stepped back and said, "Does that look like it's about halfway?"

"Give it one more little tap," I told him.

He did, and I said, "Whoa, that looks just about perfect."

"All right," he said, as he cast the ax aside. "Grab the other end of the board and let's put her in place."

After we had that accomplished, we stood back and admired our work. "What do you think?" Fred asked.

"Uh—I don't know. How does it work?"

"Can't you see? We each grab a hold of opposite ends of the board and start running in a circle. When we get to going real fast, we jump on the board at the same time and ride it as it spins around the stump."

I wasn't convinced. "Where did you hear about this thing—what was it you said you called it?"

"It's a spinning jenny."

"I understand the spinning part, but where did the jenny part come from?"

"I don't know, that's just what it's called."

"Well, who told you how to make it?"

"You know what else?" he said without answering my question.

"What?"

"Instead of two people running around the stump and then jumping on the board, they both could just go ahead and get on and let a third person push them real fast, and I bet it would just about sling you off that board."

"But wouldn't the board hit the person pushing when they stopped pushing?"

"If they was dumb enough to just stand there, I 'spect it would. But it wouldn't be hard to just get out of the way real quick after it got going real fast. You want to let's give it a try?"

I was still a little leery of that spinning jenny. "I don't know. Maybe if we done it real slow at first, you know, just run at about half as fast as we really can, then I would."

"Okay, get at your end of the board," Fred said. "And remember, when I yell 'go,' stop running and jump on. I'll do the same thing. Oh, and one more thing, when it stops we both have to get off at the same time?"

"How come?"

"'Cause if one person gets off before the other one without the other one knowing, your own weight can pull you down and you can mash your foot under the board."

When we were both in place my brother nodded, and we began running around the stump, each of us holding on to our end of the board. After about three circles Fred yelled the signal, and we both leaped simultaneously onto the board.

I expected it to spin so fast that it would make me dizzy and sling me clean off. It barely made one slow circle before it came to a stop, making a grinding sound on the surface of the stump.

We sat in dazed disappointment for a few moments. Finally Fred said, "Okay, let's get off. It didn't exactly sling us off, did it? Something's wrong."

He stood there studying the situation for a few moments before he said, "There must be something I forgot."

I certainly didn't know what it was.

Suddenly he exclaimed, "I know what it is, wait right here!"

I watched as he dashed off toward the tool shed again. In no time at all he returned with a can of axle grease in one hand and a stick in the other and began dipping a gob of the dark, heavy grease out of the can with the stick. Next, he pushed the grease into the hole where the wagon axle went through the board.

Then he smeared more grease all over the surface of the stump, and I knew I would have to find a new place to crack nuts.

When he finished he set the can of grease aside and tossed the stick off into the woods.

"All right, smarty pants," he said, "let's give it another try. And let's run harder this time before we jump on."

I didn't expect the results to be much different, so I agreed.

When we were poised at each end of the board, Fred instructed, "Same rules as before, okay?"

I agreed and we began running. I noticed right off the board was much easier to push.

"Come on, just a little faster," he yelled.

We were running almost full out when he yelled, "Go!"

When we leaped on that board it seemed to have an engine running it. I managed to hold on for two, maybe three turns, before it slung me off. I heard a yelp of pain from Fred as I went tumbling through the grass. He came limping over toward me and asked, "You okay?"

I sat up, felt of myself, and said, "Yeah, I think so. How about you?"

"My foot got smashed a little under the board when you went flying, but it's okay. That thing really took off!"

I could hear the excitement in his voice and could tell he was proud he had gotten the spinning jenny to work, in spite of the injuries we had both narrowly escaped. "I know what it needs to keep you from being slung off."

"I ain't getting back on that thing," I told him.

"Aw, come on," he implored. "What it needs is something on the board, kind of like handle bars on a bicycle, for you to hang on to."

"I don't know—that thing was flying!"

"I know it was. But I'm gonna nail a strip of wood on each end of the board so you can hang on with both hands, and I promise we'll go easy until we get the hang of it."

It didn't take us long to find two strips of hickory, strong and straight, from the woodpile. In the shed we took our father's hammer and pulled four rusty, but serviceable, nails from a board on the shed's exterior.

Once again, I held the board steady while my brother did his work. He drove two nails through each of the hickory strips and into the board, leaving room to sit on the end and hold on with both hands. I held the board up while he clinched the points of the nails underneath; then we stood back and surveyed our work.

Suddenly Fred stepped forward, put both hands on one end of the board, and said, "Stand back. Let's see how

fast it'll go with no one on it." Then he slung it as hard as
he could.

That board took off like an electric fan blade. I leaped
back in alarm as it whipped around going, "whoosh-whoosh-
whoosh."

It finally stopped and we stood there in awe. "It went
around twelve times," I said. "I counted them!"

"Now that's a spinning jenny," Fred said, all puffed up
with pride. "Let's give it another try."

"Are you plain crazy? I'm not getting back on that thing.
Next time it'll probably sling me way off yonder into the
woods."

"All right, I'll tell you what, let's just get on it while it's
sitting still, push it along real easy with our feet and kind
of get the feel of it. You'll try that, won't you?"

"Yeah, I suppose I'll try it like that."

We each headed toward opposite ends of the board.
"Remember the rules now," Fred instructed. "We both get
on and off at the same time."

When we were seated and had firm grips on the handles,
Fred said, "This feels a lot better with something to hold
on to, don't it?"

I had to admit he was correct. "Uh-huh," I nervously
replied.

We used our toes and the balls of our feet to get it moving,
and I was amazed at the ease with which the board moved
around its axis on the stump.

After a few turns, Fred said, "What do you think? You
want to try it with a running start again?"

I did feel much better about the thing now that I had

something to hold on to, so I agreed to give it another go.

We were both running hard and fast when Fred shouted out the signal to get on board. As soon as we jumped on, the spinning jenny seemed to have a power source of its own as it whipped us around the stump. I hung on for dear life and felt as if I would be lifted off the board and laid straight out in the air and slung off out into a nearby tree top if I dared let go of the handle.

When the jenny finally slowed to a stop, we dizzily stumbled off the board and collapsed breathlessly onto the ground.

Fred was the first to speak. Between heaving breaths, he said, "That was great! I can't believe how fast it went! Did you count the times we went around?"

"No, I was too busy trying to hold on. But I guess at least fifteen."

Fred sat up and yelled out to the world, "We got us a spinning jenny!" Then he turned to me and said, "You ready to go again?"

"Shoot yeah, let's see if we can get it going faster this time."

The spinning jenny turned out to be the best thing my brother had built or invented so far. And for a while it was the number one thing on our list to do when we got home from school and on every opportunity we had on weekends. But then it turned into a nightmare.

CHAPTER THREE

GOING FISHING

The word got out about the spinning jenny and it wasn't long before our cousins, our friends, and their cousins were all coming in droves.

We had discovered that if two riders got on, and a third person, preferably a strong and fast one, pushed the board around as hard as they could and jumped clean at the last second, then the spinning jenny would sling all but the most tenacious off the board, making it a contest to see who could stay on and who would be slung off.

It was used so much a round trench was worn in the ground underneath the ends of the board.

Soon there were crushed toes, skinned elbows and knees, heads conked when someone fell off instead of being slung off, and fights over who was going to ride it next.

Fred decided we were going to initiate a charge to ride, but before he could implement his toll, one of our cousins broke an arm.

Her parents, along with others, descended upon our momma with numerous complaints until one Saturday afternoon she marched out to the spinning jenny with my brother Ned and had him pull the plank off the stump and deposit it under the house.

And that was the end of the spinning jenny, which was all right with me. The thrill of it had diminished, and the only thing I regretted was that my friend Poudlum Robinson hadn't had an opportunity to ride it.

I hadn't seen Poudlum for a while. That was because he was black and we didn't go to the same school. Since the warmth of summer had faded, I had only seen him a couple of times on weekends over at Miss Lena's Store.

The store was halfway between his house and mine, so we met there sometimes and had us both a peach-flavored Nehi soda and an ice cream sandwich. We used the money we had secretly stashed away back during the summer. It was the reward we had given ourselves after discovering an illegal whiskey-making operation and the bootlegger's cache of cash in a hollow tree way back in the woods on Satilfa Creek.

Thanksgiving weekend was coming up and Poudlum and I had planned weeks ago to spend it camping out at a fishing hole on that same creek.

My momma wasn't too keen on the idea, but when I came home from school with the first prize for the Thanksgiving Poem, she relented and gave her permission.

My fifth-grade teacher had assigned everyone to write a poem about what they were thankful for. We had to turn them in on Tuesday, and on Wednesday afternoon before we were dismissed for the long weekend, she announced she was going to recite the winning poem.

I just about fell out of my seat when she began reading
my Thanksgiving Poem:

I'm thankful for dressing and gravy
And the boys serving in the Navy
I'm thankful for turkey and ham
And for tough old Uncle Sam
I'm thankful for squash casserole
And for the heroes of old
I'm thankful for pecan pie
And for the beautiful sky
I'm thankful for bread and butter
And for my two brothers
I'm thankful for sweet potato pie
And for being old enough not to cry
I'm thankful for sweet ice tea
And for the opportunity to just be
I'm thankful for green beans and butter beans
And for all the children and the teens
I'm thankful for lemon glazed pound cake
And for being able to swim in the lake
I'm thankful for potato salad
And for the numbers when my friends are tallied
I'm thankful for being physically sustained
And for the grace of being spiritually without blame

The teacher gave me an A-plus and wrote a note to my
momma on my poem informing her I had won first place.
I could tell by the look on Momma's face when she read it
that I could go camping for a week if I wanted to.

Poudlum and I planned to meet at Miss Lena's Store on Friday after Thanksgiving Day, right after our noon meal. That way we would have time to walk to the Cypress Hole on the Satilfa, set up camp, and get in some fishing before it got dark. I just hoped he had done something to make his momma happy, too.

Thanksgiving Day came and went. Since my daddy was gone we all went to Aunt Cleo's and Uncle Elmer's house and ate turkey and all the trimmings with them.

On Friday, I was anxious to get going. My momma served up big bowls of steaming vegetable soup with corn bread and buttermilk, which was a welcome change from all the rich food the day before.

While I was sopping up the dregs of the soup with a piece of cornbread, she was fixing me a bag of biscuits left over from breakfast. She would bore a hole into them with her finger and pour the hole full of Blue Ribbon cane syrup, pinch the hole closed, and then wrap them up in waxed paper.

"These biscuits will fill you up in case you and Poudlum don't catch any fish," she said. "But I 'spect y'all will, cause black folks know how to fish. I want y'all to be real careful around that water now," she concluded as she began packing my stuff into a small cotton picking sack.

She had allowed me to take one of her old skillets, a small one, along with an old quilt, a box of matches, a packet of salt, some cornmeal, and a half-pint jar filled with lard to fry the fish in.

"You got your pocketknife?" she asked.

"Yes, ma'am, and Ned sharpened it real good for me this

morning so I can scale them fish and clean them properly," I said as I slipped the strap of the sack over my shoulder.

My momma hugged me and said, "Now remember, if y'all get too cold or hungry just go to your Uncle Curtis's house. It's not too far from the creek."

The strap of the sack was cutting into my shoulder before I got to the store. I hoped Poudlum's load was lighter so we could take turns carrying mine. The only thing I had told him to bring was a quilt and some fish hooks.

He was nowhere in sight when I arrived at the store, so I set my sack by the steps at the front door, went in, and started gathering some supplies just in case the fish weren't biting. I didn't want to be stuck in the woods hungry with nothing except biscuits to eat.

We planned to be there two nights, so I counted the meals in my mind while I selected cans of Vienna sausage, sardines, potted meat, pork and beans, and four dime boxes of saltines. We didn't have to worry about anything to drink; we could just drink water from the creek.

"Good Lord," Lena cried out when I piled it all on the counter. "Son, what you planning to with all this stuff?"

"Me and Poudlum gonna camp out and fish on the creek. This stuff is just in case we don't catch any fish."

After she bagged it all up I paid her and went outside and stuffed it all into my sack even as I became concerned about the weight of it.

I looked down Center Point Road, shading my eyes from the sun with my hand, and saw no sign of Poudlum. I hated the thought that I might have to walk all the way over to his house and try to convince Mrs. Robinson to let him go, but

I knew Lena would watch my stuff if I did.

After waiting about half an hour I went back into the store and got myself a Nehi and sat on the front steps nursing it while I gazed down the dirt road looking for my friend.

I began to wonder what I would do if he didn't come. Just go on by myself or go back home and share all the stuff in my sack with my brothers?

I didn't think I wanted to sleep on the bank of the Satilfa by myself, but still, I didn't want to give up.

Miss Lena came outside and stayed on the steps with me. "You think maybe Poudlum isn't coming?" she asked softly.

"I don't know, but it's not like him not to at least come tell me if he's not."

After another thirty minutes I got angry and defiant. I stood up, shouldered my sack and started walking down Center Point Road toward the creek. Over my shoulder, I called back to Miss Lena, "I'm going fishing, and I'll be at the Cypress Hole if anybody's looking for me."

I had to stop and rest twice before I got to the Church. Even though I kept switching my sack from shoulder to shoulder, the strap bit painfully into it as I walked, and it grew heavier and heavier with each step I took.

The sun was still beaming warmth down when I crossed the Mill Creek Bridge. Halfway up the hill beyond it I could see the sun striking gold from the mica stones in the ditch.

That was about the time I heard the ruckus coming from back behind me. Somebody was yelling. I cocked my head, listened real hard and heard a faint voice yelling, "Mister Ted, wait up, I'm a comin'!"

I recognized my friend's voice and was elated that he was coming after all. The day took on a whole new outlook as my excitement about the venture returned. I stepped off the road, set my sack down in the shade of a big black gum tree, and waited.

It wasn't long before Poudlum came trotting up with a wet sheen on his face. He stopped in the middle of the road when he saw me and said, "Hey, Mister Ted."

"I done told you I ain't no mister. I'm just Ted."

"I keeps forgettin'. But anyway, I'm here, even if I is late."

"What happened to you? I waited forever on you."

"We got company. Dey been here all week, and my momma thought I ought not to run off and leave my cousins. But I finally got her away from all dem folks and told her dat I had promised Mister Ted we was going fishing. She thinks a lot of you, so when I mentions yo' name she packed up a syrup bucket full of biscuits and side meat and told me to git. When I got to de store Miss Lena told me you had already started down de road. I been walking real fast and running some to catch up wid you."

I was so happy to see Poudlum that I didn't care about the details of his tardiness; I was just pleased that he was finally with me.

"What you got in your sack besides a syrup bucket full of biscuits?"

"I got some fishing line, some hooks, and some corks."

"That don't sound heavy at all. Mine's about to cut through my shoulder. Would you carry it a while for me and I'll carry yours?"

"Shore I will," Poudlum said as he shouldered my sack. "Lawd, what you gots in it, rocks?"

We stopped to rest again a ways on down the road, secured our bags in some tall weeds, climbed down a steep bank, and drank our fill from a spring we knew about. The water was cool, crystal clear, and sweet to the taste as it came bubbling up out of the ground. It was only about two inches deep, and as I lay on my belly I could see sunlight reflecting gold glints off the sand beneath the water.

We rested for a while before we got back on the road, anxious to begin our adventure on the creek. But we hadn't gone far before Poudlum began asking questions.

"Dis fishing hole we heading for, de Cypress Hole, colored folks ain't usually allowed to fish at it. Why you think dat is?"

That was a perplexing question and I wasn't sure how to answer it, but after a little thought I told Poudlum, "I think it's 'cause they 'fraid y'all would catch all the fish in it." I knew it wasn't the real answer, but I didn't know how to say the real reason without hurting his feelings. I think he knew the real reason, but I could tell he appreciated my answer as the way I felt, because he grinned and said, "Why you 'spect it's called de Cypress Hole?"

"Probably 'cause there's a lot of cypress trees around it."

"De water deep in it?"

"There's a big deep place right below the shoals, which

is the Cypress Hole. That's where we'll fish."

"What's a shoal?"

"Uh, that's a place in a stream where the water is running over a lot of rocks. We can walk across the creek on those rocks. That's what we'll do when we set out our trot line."

"What kinda fish you think we gonna catch?"

"Catfish and perch, that's all there is in there."

"What we gon use for bait?"

"We'll catch some crickets and grasshoppers when we get there. Plus there's some dead pine trees we can get grub worms out of. I brought a little empty pint jar we can put them in."

"What if you fished without no bait?"

"You mean just throw an empty fish hook in the water?

"Uh-huh."

"Wouldn't nothing happen, Poudlum. Why, that would be kind of like licking a clean plate."

There was a little swampy area about a quarter of a mile before we got to the Satilfa where a big stand of bamboo grew. We stopped there and cut us some fishing poles. We cut four in case we happened to break one, plus we planned to use some of the joints in the bamboo to make whistles out of later while we sat around the fire.

I used the small blade of my pocketknife to cut the poles down because I wanted to keep the big blade sharp to clean the fish with.

Once we had cut the tops off and stripped the poles clean, Poudlum carried them and his sack while I took my turn carrying my heavier sack.

A little further up the road I knew the Satilfa Creek Bridge would come into sight just around the next curve.

When we rounded that curve we both stopped and stared for a moment because there was a vehicle in the road up ahead.

I squinted my eyes and recognized my Uncle Curvin's old pickup truck. It had a jack under the front of it with the truck lifted up off the ground. My uncle had had a flat tire.

At that moment he appeared from around the back of the truck rolling his spare tire. He wasn't having an easy time because my uncle was crippled from a war wound.

"Dat looks like yo' Uncle Curvin up ahead," Poudlum said.

"Yeah, that's him. Looks like he got a flat."

"He look like he so skinny it would take two of him just to make a shadow."

"Yeah, he's skinny all right," I said. "He's also crippled. Let's go give him a hand."

My uncle was mighty proud to see us. We loosened the lug nuts on his flat tire, replaced it with his spare and jacked his truck down for him.

"Thank you, boys," he said. "Y'all heading for the Cypress Hole to do some fishing?"

"Yes, sir," I told him. "We gonna camp out and fish for a couple of nights. Where you coming from?"

"I been up to Grove Hill, and, Lord have mercy, boys, a terrible thing happened there this morning, with me right slap dab in the middle of it!"

CHAPTER FOUR

THE CYPRESS HOLE

P oudlum and I both thought a lot of my Uncle Curvin. We had picked cotton for him back during the summer and he had always been mighty good to us. We also admired him because he had fought in World War One all the way over in Europe and got himself shot in the leg, which crippled him but did entitle him to a small disability check that came in the mail each month from the government.

He looked the same as always, wearing his old brown slouch hat with sweat stains on it, a blue, long-sleeved work shirt, and a pair of overalls. Beneath his hat, his face was all caved in because he didn't have any teeth.

"What in the world happened up there, Uncle Curvin?" I asked.

"I went up there to cash my check at the bank and all heck broke loose while Mrs. Vinny was counting out my money. She was telling me how she wanted to buy a bushel of sweet taters when all of a sudden she stopped talking and her eyes got big as saucers. I could tell she was looking at something behind me, so I turned around. You boys won't never believe what I was looking at!"

"We might, if you would just tell us. What was it?" I asked.

"Scared me worsen I been scared since I was in the war. Came might near wetting my pants on myself. I been shaking like a leaf in a windstorm ever since."

"Shore sound like it wuz something real bad," Poudlum said.

"Yeah, maybe we'll find out what it was one of these days," I said with a sideways glance toward Poudlum, but my words were directed toward my uncle to let him know we were getting a bit impatient.

Uncle Curvin sank down on the running board of his truck like he was worn down to a frazzle. Whatever had happened to him, it had just about got the best of him.

"Y'all just keep your britches on and I'll tell what it was I saw when I turned around."

We stepped closer and squatted down in front of him in anticipation.

"When I turned around, boys, I was looking down both barrels of a sawed-off double-barreled twelve-gauge shotgun. And it was scary, 'cause I knew that thing could scatter me to kingdom come."

"Good Lord, Uncle Curvin!" I exclaimed. "Was it a bank robber?"

"They was two of them," he said. "The other one had a mean-looking pistol that he was waving around."

"What did you do, Mister Curvin?" Poudlum asked, wide-eyed as an owl at dusk dark.

"Why, I did exactly what he told me to. I got face down on the floor and started praying."

"They told you to pray?" I asked.

"Naw, I done that on my own."

"Then what happened?"

"Well, the one with the scattergun held everybody at bay while the other one went behind the counter and cleaned out all the money. I peeked up and saw that my little pile of money was still laying on the counter.

"The one with the pistol grabbed it when he came out from behind the counter with his sack of money, but the other one jerked it out of his hand and dropped it down on the floor next to me on their way out of the bank."

"So you didn't lose your money?"

"Nary a dime of it. Got it all right here in the bib pocket of my overalls. I don't know why they done that, but I shore do appreciate them not taking my pitiful little pension. A lot of rich folks can afford to lose a lot of money more than I can afford to lose these few dollars."

"Did they catch 'em, Mister Curvin?"

"Naw, they got clean away. Wouldn't nobody to stop 'em."

"How about the law?" I asked.

"Shoot, the law was all out collecting their cut from the bootleggers. Mr. Leon Stringer, he owns the bank you know, went running outside after the robbers left with his necktie and suit coat flapping in the wind and went straight over to the sheriff's office, but couldn't find nobody there except the jailer. That's what he told us when he come back. That sorry excuse for a sheriff, Elroy Crowe, showed up 'bout a half hour later, just long enough for the trail to get cold."

"Sounds like dem bank robbers got clean away," Poudlum said.

"Well, somebody did see 'em leave town heading down
Highway 84 toward Coffeeville. Sheriff Crowe got on his
radio and had somebody put up a road block down there
to stop them from taking the ferry across the Tombigbee
River, 'cause he said they were probably trying to get across
the Mississippi State Line."

"Did they get across the river?" I asked.

"Naw. I heard everything on the sheriff's radio. They
skidded around when they come up on the road block and
headed back up Highway 84. They found their abandoned
vehicle 'side the bridge over the Satilfa Creek, and figured
they were heading down the creek toward the river on foot.
Last I heard they were talking about getting some dogs
together and start tracking them."

"Whew, you done had yourself a day, Uncle Curvin. You
saw a bank robbery, and then on top of that, had yourself
a flat tire."

He got up off the running board and started getting in
his truck when he said, "You got that right, son. I believe
I'm going home and lay down for a spell. I ain't used to bank
robbers and flat tires."

He cranked up his truck, put it in gear, leaned out the
window and said, "How long you boys plan to fish?"

"Tonight and tomorrow night, and then we'll probably
go home Sunday morning," I told him.

"I might mosey over here and check on y'all sometime
this weekend."

"We'll be at the Cypress Hole, and we got two extra poles. Come on by."

"I expect I might. Good luck, boys," he called out through the truck window as he pulled out onto the road. We watched until his dust trail disappeared around the curve.

Poudlum scratched his head and said, "You don't think he made all dat stuff up, do you?"

"Naw, he wouldn't do that. Come on, the trail to the Cypress Hole is right up yonder on the left."

"Well, I just hopes dem bank robbers did head down de creek towards de river and not back up de creek dis way."

"They probably want to get to Mississippi, like the sheriff said. They wouldn't come back up this way," I reassured him.

We could see the bridge over the creek when we turned off the road onto the trail that angled through the woods to our destination. On both sides of the trail there were great red oaks and cedar trees, thick with tangled muscadine vines. The wild grapes had long ago been consumed by squirrels and raccoons. I liked those wild grapes. You could pop one in your mouth, bite down on it and it would burst in your mouth and render a sweet, tangy juice. There were seeds which you had to spit out, and the hull, after you chewed on it a little. My momma made some delicious jelly from the juice of them. She even made preserves from the hulls. They were both tasty inside a biscuit.

The trail was like a tunnel with tree branches forming a canopy above your head. A little further into the woods and the cypress trees began to appear with long draping ribbons of Spanish moss hanging from the limbs.

"Dis is spooky," Poudlum uttered in almost a whisper.

"Don't worry," I said. "It opens up into a big clearing just a little ways up on the creek bank."

We emerged from the trail and there it was, the place where Ned and Fred and I swam in the summer and the best fishing hole on the creek. You could see the sky up through a large opening of the forest.

Poudlum turned in a complete circle, taking it all in. "Now, I likes dis place," he said. "It's big and open. And look over there, it looks like somebody had a fire built over by de creek bank."

What he was referring to was a circle of big round creek rocks, blackened with soot, where the previous campers had built their fire.

The sound of the water was the best part. It swept gurgling and churning over the flat rocks of the shoals before dropping into the pool below. That pool was where the fish were.

Poudlum noticed, too. "Dat water spilling over dem rocks shore do sound fine. It soothes you kind of like when my momma sings a hymn at night."

"Yeah, I like the way it sounds too. We'll sleep real fine tonight listening to it. But first we have some work to do. Let's set our sacks down and start gathering firewood. We'll need a big stack of it so we can keep the fire going all night. It'll get cold soon as the sun goes down."

We stashed our stuff next to the fire bed and began dragging and carrying limbs and sticks out of the surrounding woods. Soon we had enough to last us through the night and into the cold morning.

We even found a long-dead loblolly pine, which had rotted away except for the heart that had turned into lighter wood. We broke it into pieces knowing all we had to do was stick a lit match to it and it would blaze up because of the turpentine in it.

There was also an abundant supply of lighter knots, the remnants of where the branches had been attached to the trunk. They looked like an elbow and were handy to throw on a bed of coals that had died down, to get a quick blaze going again.

The next item on our agenda was to gather some fish bait. Poudlum had that covered. "I passed a big dead pine tree over yonder that's about half rotten and I could hear dem sawyers inside it."

Sawyers were fat, round, white grub worms with two little red pincers on their head, which they used to eat dead pine trees. And Poudlum was correct, you could hear them inside of a dead tree if you listened real close. They made a kind of steady smacking sound. I supposed it was them eating wood that made the sound. I never knew why they were called what they were, but figured it was because they were actually sawing the dead log up with those little pincers on their head. What I did know was that catfish loved them, and so did perch.

When we got to the tree we pulled the loose bark off the trunk in hunks and dug the fat grubs out of the rotten wood until we had our jar almost full.

"How many you think we got, Poudlum?"

"I 'spect about fifty. You think dat's enough?"

"Yeah, that's plenty for tonight. Crumble up a handful

of rotten wood and put in the jar so they'll have something to eat."

After Poudlum screwed the cap on the jar I took the small blade of my knife and jabbed a few air holes into it.

It was still warm, but I knew the air would take on a chill as soon as the sun went behind the trees. It was time to set up our trot line. Poudlum held the ball of cord on the bank, and after I had slipped off my shoes and socks, I rolled up my pants legs and waded through the swift running water toward the other side of the creek with my end of the cord. Then I pulled out a little extra slack so I would have enough cord to tie it to a tree. Now that I had measured the length of cord we would need, I returned to where Poudlum was holding the other end.

"What do we do next?" Poudlum asked.

"Unravel about six more feet so it'll have enough slack to go past the shoal and drop into the pool below it."

We stretched our measured cord out across the clearing on the ground. Then we cut a bunch of two-foot pieces of cord and got down on our knees and tied the short cords every few feet along the length of our trot line. Then we went back and attached a fish hook and a small lead sinker on the end of each short piece of cord. It was tedious work, but it was a good way to catch a lot of fish.

We stood back and admired our work. "Nothing left to do except bait the hooks," I told Poudlum. "Then we'll stretch it out across the creek, tie both ends to trees and drop it over into the deep water."

The fat worms wiggled and attempted to bite us with their tiny pincers when we stuck them with the fish hooks.

"You 'spect dat hurts 'em when we sticks 'em?" Poudlum asked.

"Naw, they just worms."

"Den how come dey twists around and wiggles so?"

"I don't know. Probably it's just a reflex or something like that. Come on, let's get 'em in the water while they're still wiggling so they'll attract the fish."

We tied one end of the trot line to a stump near the creek bank on our side, and once again, I crossed over, but this time I secured the end to a tree and watched as the water washed the line over into the deep pool.

"How you tells when a fish gets on it?"

"You can't," I said while I was getting my shoes and socks back on. "We'll just have to run it ever so often. We'll do it just before dark so if any fish are on it we'll have time to clean them. After that we'll put more bait on if we need to and run it again in the morning."

We rigged up our cane poles with hooks, lines, and sinkers, baited the hooks and settled down on the side of the creek to fish in the fading light of the day.

The gurgle of the water coupled with the surrounding solitude created the exact atmosphere we had been yearning for, and we knew then that all our planning, cajoling, walking, and work had been worth it.

The trees had lost most of their leaves and the fading light filtered through the branches and played light games on the water's surface as our corks bobbed listlessly on the ever-changing silver liquid of the dark pool we gazed into.

Something was not as it should be.

I shook off the hypnotic feeling and realized that Poudlum's cork was what was missing. It had disappeared beneath the surface and the only thing visible was the straight line going into the water.

"Poudlum!" I cried out. "You got one! Hold on tight to your pole!"

"Good Lawd!" Poudlum exclaimed as he stood up and got a good grip on his pole. "It feels like a big one, too!"

We threw several back, but when we quit just before dark we had four fat catfish and three perch as wide as your hand. I began cleaning them and had them ready to fry by the time Poudlum got a fire going.

"It's just about dark," Poudlum said. "Don't you think it's about time we run dat trot line?"

While I was removing my shoes in preparation to check the trot line, I glanced across the creek, lowered my head, then jerked it back up.

Had something moved over there? I strained my eyes, but the light was beginning to fade.

A peculiar feeling swept over me. I put my feet back in my shoes and told Poudlum we would wait until the morning to check the trot line.

I also asked him to put some more wood on the fire.

CHAPTER FIVE

THE VISITORS

"I put some hickory on after I got the fire going real good. It makes the hottest coals," Poudlum said as he used a stick to rake a pile of red-hot, glowing coals from beneath the flames. "Put de skillet on dem and I guarantee they'll fry up our fish."

I spooned some lard into the black skillet and placed it on the hot embers. The cleaned fish were all wet and glistening on a big flat rock I had fetched from the creek. By the time I got them coated with a mixture of cornmeal, salt, and pepper Momma had mixed up for me, the grease was spitting and popping.

The aroma of the fresh fish frying made Poudlum and me lick our lips in anticipation. "Um-mmm," he moaned while he spread a big brown paper bag out for the cooked fish to be placed on.

When I finished there were eight catfish filets and three big bream, all browned with a crusty coating of cornmeal.

"Now dis is what it's all about," Poudlum said as he munched away.

I had to agree with him. It was mighty fine fish. In spite of the amazing good taste, we could eat only half of them. "We'll save de rest of 'em for breakfast," Poudlum said as he carefully wrapped the remainder of the fish. "Better keep them here close to de fire so no varmints get to 'em."

We washed our greasy hands in the swift water and stood by the fire with our palms spread wide to dry them.

Darkness had set in and the forest, along with the creek, had turned to blackness. Even though it was only a few feet away, the sound of the water was the only thing that indicated the creek existed.

"I'm gon stoke up dis fire some so we got some light, and den does you wants to play some mumblety-peg?"

"Yeah, I would, but it'll dull our knife blades and we need to keep them sharp to clean fish with."

"I brought along a little whet rock," Poudlum said. "I can sharpen 'em up again."

"All right," I agreed as I smoothed out a place on the ground next to the fire with my hands. "Whoever gets twelve points first wins."

Mumblety-peg is a game in which the players flip a knife, the object being to stick the blade or blades firmly in the ground so it doesn't fall over. The big blade is opened fully and the small blade is opened halfway forming an "L" shape by the blades. The player flips the knife, and if it sticks into the ground by the small blade only, it counts as three points, or two points if it sticks by the big blade, and one point if it sticks by both blades. No points are scored if neither sticks, and the flip passes to the next player.

But before either of us scored twelve points, we got

drowsy. We gave up on the game and got our quilts and rolled up in them by the fire.

"Hey, Poudlum."

"Uh-huh," he answered sleepily.

"Anytime you wake up during the night, throw a little more wood on the fire and I'll do the same."

The moon kept appearing and reappearing as it butted clouds around in the sky like a billy goat. A million stars were twinkling away in the heavens above just before I closed my eyes and succumbed to the warmth of our fire and my momma's quilt.

I don't know how long I had been asleep when I began to feel something hard jabbing me through the quilt. I woke up to see a hot bed of coals glowing in the fire and thought I was just dreaming. Then I felt the jabbing again. It was rough and hard this time and I knew it was real.

I turned over, sat up, and in the dim light looked up and saw what I knew had to be the same sight that had frightened my uncle earlier in the day.

It was the black, glaring bore holes of a sawed-off double-barreled shotgun.

"Wake up, boy," a gruff voice said.

There were two of them. The other one was stoking up the fire and adding wood to it. I could see him out of the corner of my eye, but my attention was focused on the two black holes above my head, which I knew could belch out fire and death.

After I raised up on my elbow, he said, "Go on, sit up now. We just want to talk to you."

Fresh flames were licking up from the hot coals around

the firewood the other one had added, and a flickering, shadowy light was beginning to illuminate our campsite.

I sat up, drawing my quilt around me like some kind of cloak of protection, but it didn't help. The man reached down, grabbed it off me and tossed it aside.

His shoes and pants legs were sopping wet halfway up to his knees. The other one's were too. I knew then that they had waded across the creek from the other side, and that my eyes hadn't been playing tricks on me earlier.

I was on my knees now. He had on a long-sleeved denim jacket and looked like he hadn't shaved in about a week. His eyes were beady as a squirrel's as they darted around from under the brim of a felt hat from which long hair spilled out and hung down to his shoulders.

I knew who they were. They were the bank robbers, but I was awake enough to realize they probably didn't know I knew that.

"What y'all want, mister?" I managed to say.

"We just want to warm ourselves by y'all's fire and dry our wet shoes. You don't mind if we do that, do you?"

"No, sir. Don't mind at all."

"What's your name, boy?" the one with the scattergun asked.

"My name's Ted."

"What's your little nigger friend's name?"

I didn't like them calling him that, but I went ahead and told them Poudlum's name. He was just now waking up and his eyes were wide and white, like two hen eggs in a pool of soot.

There was a bond of friendship and loyalty between

Poudlum and me. We had encountered dangerous situations before, and we could communicate with just our eyes. I gave him a look, and I could tell he understood we shouldn't let on that we knew who our visitors were.

The other man, the one who had stoked up the fire, was standing over next to Poudlum. He just had on a thin cotton shirt, and I could see he was shivering in the cold. His hair was short and curly and he had a clean-looking round, baby-face that looked like he was almost too young to shave. He was bareheaded, but he had some mean-looking eyes underneath his bushy brows.

Since introductions were in order, I boldly asked, "Who might y'all be, sir?"

The one with the shotgun grinned and sparks shot out of his mouth as the fire reflected off a gold tooth he had. "My name's Jesse, and that's my brother Frank over there."

They both began snickering when he said that, like somebody had told a joke or something.

"You boys don't mind if we sit down by the fire here and dry ourselves out, do you," Jesse said as he eased down to the ground and began taking off his wet shoes.

"No, sir, we don't mind at all. We happy to share it with y'all."

They put their wet shoes up close to the fire, squeezed the water out of their socks and placed them on the hot, round rocks surrounding it.

As steam began to rise from the wet socks, Jesse said, "How come Poudlum don't say nothing? Is he mute or something?"

I wanted to tell him I could ask the same question about

Frank, but that might have seemed like a smart-aleck answer, so I refrained. Instead, I said, "He's just a sleepyhead, hard to wake up."

"How about that, Poudlum? Jesse asked. "Can you talk, boy?"

"Yes, sir," Poudlum replied.

Frank finally spoke up when he said, "We proud to hear you can talk, Poudlum. Now, hand me that bag of fried fish y'all had left from supper. Pass it over here, 'cause we mighty hungry."

When Poudlum passed the grease-stained bag to Frank, we had eye contact again, and at that time we both knew Jesse and Frank had been watching us for a while.

They ate our breakfast like starving men, wolfing down the fish without chewing or even tasting the freshness of it.

Jesse belched, and said, "Mighty nice of y'all to share your supper with us, boys."

"Is you gentlemen out here in de woods hunting?" Poudlum asked.

"Yeah, we coon hunting," Frank said, and they both smirked with amusement.

Poudlum wasn't fazed. "Where y'all's coon dogs?"

It was Jesse's turn to make a joke. "Our dogs? Oh, we lost our dogs," he said while they both about fell in the creek laughing.

They didn't know we knew the source of their merriment, and I wanted to keep it that way.

They stopped laughing and got serious. "We got us a problem here, boys," Jesse said.

"How's that, Mister Jesse?" I asked.

"We need to get us some sleep."

"I don't see how that's a problem. Y'all are welcome to just stretch out by our fire and doze right off."

"Yeah, while you and Poudlum light out of here," Frank said.

"We camping out here for the weekend," I said. "And we got a lot more fishing to do. We're not going anywhere."

"You got that right," Jesse said. "I got an idea, Frank," Jesse continued, ignoring us.

"What you got in mind?"

"Get that ball of cord they made the trot line with out of Poudlum's sack and I'll show you."

They had been watching us since way before dark!

Frank, following instructions from Jesse, used the cord to tie loops around both mine and Poudlum's thumbs. Jesse took the two ends leading from mine and tied them to his big toe. Frank did the same with Poudlums's.

"Now, let's all lay down close to the fire and get us some shut-eye," Jesse said. "We been coon hunting' all day and we're plumb tuckered out."

"Wouldn't be nothin' left of a coon if you shot him with that big old shotgun," Poudlum piped up.

"Don't you worry about it, boy. Y'all lay down like I told you," Jesse sharply replied.

After that everybody stretched out next to the fire and things got real quiet, the only sounds being the crackling of the fire and the gushing of the creek.

I looked at my thumbs and knew I couldn't get my knife out of my pocket without pulling Jesse's big toe and alerting him. I figured they just wanted to rest and would let us go in the morning.

Poudlum's voice jarred me from my thoughts when he said, "Mister Jesse?"

"What now, boy?" Jesse growled.

"Y'all been over 'cross de creek for a spell just watching us?"

"Why you think that, boy?"

"'Cause you knowed where de cord was we made de trot line with."

"Well now, ain't you a smart little nigger?"

"Why didn't y'all just come on 'cross de creek earlier?"

"Because if you boys had seen us coming, you would have run off and told somebody you seen us, and we can't have that," Jesse said.

"How come we do dat? Y'all just hunting coons."

Frank's voice came harshly across the fire. "If you don't shut him up Jesse, then I will."

"Listen, Poudlum, you little chatter-mouth nigger, I'm gonna take that cord off Frank's toe, tie it to a big rock, throw it in the creek and watch it pull you down by your thumbs if you say another word."

I realized that Poudlum was attempting to find out their intentions, and that it was time I helped him out. "He don't mean no harm, Mister Jesse," I said. "He's just bad about asking a lot of questions. I was just wondering too, do y'all intend to continue hunting coons tomorrow morning?"

"Hey!" Jesse raised his head up and said. "What I just told your friend goes for you, too."

"All right, Mister Jesse, I'll be quiet, but I just wondered

what you gentlemen gonna do with us tomorrow morning."

Jesse sat back up and told Frank to put some more wood
on the fire. "I do believe these boys know something they
ain't telling us. We gonna get it out of them before we get
some sleep."

The fire flamed up and soon there was enough light to
see the outline of everybody's face. I looked around and
was able to see the flickering reflection of the flames in
everybody's eyes.

The ones in Jesse's surely reminded me of the devil, and
when he spoke I was afraid not to answer truthfully.

"You boys know who we are, don't you? If you lie to me
I'm gonna hold your heads underwater in that cold creek
for a while. Now, tell me who you think we are!"

He was looking directly at me and I could almost feel the
dark, cold creek water sucking me down. I groped for words,
and finally blurted out, "Y'all are the bank robbers!"

"Tell us how you know that, boy."

After I told them the story Uncle Curvin had told us,
Jesse said, "Well, now that's better, to have everything out
in the open. Honesty is always the best policy, boys."

Frank was snickering on the other side of the fire.

"Everybody thought y'all would be hightailing it toward
the Tombigbee, trying to get to the Mississippi state line,"
Poudlum said.

"Of course they did, but a smart man always does the
opposite of what his adversaries expect. Remember that,
boys, it's my little contribution toward your education,"
Jesse said.

"How y'all outfox dem dogs?" Poudlum asked.

"That was easy," Frank gloated. "When we left the car we went down the bank of this creek a good way, leaving a trail. After going a good ways, we got in the water and doubled back past the bridge and the car and come on up this way. I figure the dogs are all the way to the Tombigbee River by now, sniffing around for tracks they ain't never gonna find."

"What about in the morning?" I asked again.

Jesse answered, "We'll worry about that in the morning. Right now we all going to sleep. I'm more tired than a dead mule. No more talking. Lay down." It got real quiet around the fire and I was just about to drift off when I heard Poudlum whisper softly, "What y'all do wid de money?"

Although sleep was almost upon me, just before I succumbed to it I heard Frank respond with a whispered riddle: "It's wet but it's dry, it's deep but it's nearby."

Chapter Six

HELD CAPTIVE

A thick morning mist hung over the creek and rays of pale light were beginning to sift through the tree branches from the east when I first roused up. I could hear the water moving under the blanket of fog and the croaking of a frog from his perch on a wet rock somewhere out in the creek. I was in that state between sleep and wakefulness. It was that in between place where things seemed real, but you couldn't touch them or move them, only be aware of them.

It was a soothing place to be if you were warm and comfortable in your own feather bed, a place where you wanted to linger as long as you could. But if you were cold, stiff, and not quite sure where you were it faded rapidly.

A rustling sound off in the woods brought me fully awake. I sat up and started to raise my hands to rub my eyes, but something was holding them down.

"Hey, boy, what you trying to do, pull my toe off?"

It all came flooding back, the memory of last night and the predicament Poudlum and I were in. That's when I saw the flash of silver slashing through the early morning light. It was Jesse's knife as he cut the cord connecting my thumbs to his big toe.

"There you go, boy, you loose now."

His voice was low and gravelly, a morning voice, but it didn't stay that way. When he looked across the bed of ashes that had been the fire and saw Frank asleep alone he got up, rushed over and began shaking his partner. "Wake up!" he shouted.

Frank sat up like a jack-in-the-box. "What? What is it?" he said as he scrambled around looking for danger.

"Poudlum's gone! How did he get away?"

"I-I-I don't know!" Frank stuttered. "I didn't feel nothing during the night!"

"How long you think he's been gone?"

"I don't know that either. Long enough, I 'spect."

"He could've been gone all night and be bringing the law in here right now," Jesse moaned as he turned and gazed off in all directions as if he expected a posse to come charging in at any moment.

Frank was staring at the frayed end of the cord leading from his big toe. "Looks like he chewed through it like some kind of rat or something."

They both turned their attention toward me. "Where you think he went off to?" Jesse barked.

I remembered the rustling sound I had heard when I still wasn't quite awake. "I figure he woke up cold and just went to get us some more firewood," I said.

"Dat's exactly where I been," Poudlum called out from the tree line where he stood with an armload of wood.

Frank scrambled up off the ground like it was on fire, and Jesse spun around toward the direction of Poudlum's voice with his hands and arms held out in front of him like he needed to protect himself from something.

When he saw Poudlum, he said, "Good Lord, boy, you just about scared the wits out of me. How long you been up?"

"Just long enough to rustle up dis wood and a few lighter knots."

"How did you get loose?"

"Bit dat cord in two."

"Why did you do that?"

"'Cause I was real cold and we needed some wood, but I didn't want to wake none of y'all up," Poudlum replied while he walked over and dropped his load of fuel next to the cold fire.

"How come you didn't run off?" Jesse asked.

Poudlum knelt by the smoldering coals and placed two pine knots in the center of them and began stacking wood on top. When he finished he drug a wooden match out of his pocket and raked the head of it across one of the rocks surrounding the fire bed. After it flamed up he tossed it in the center. It caught and little flames began licking up toward the fresh fuel.

"Well?" Jesse insisted. "How come?"

I could tell the bank robbers were slightly stunned when they just stood there with their mouths open when Poudlum said, "'Cause I wouldn't never run off and leave my friend here all by hisself in a pickle like we is in. No, sir, I wouldn't never do dat."

I wasn't sure what Jesse and Frank thought about what Poudlum had said, but it made me realize how fortunate I was to have a great friend like him. The fire was blazing up now and the heat from it warmed my body, but not as much as Poudlum's words had warmed my heart.

Jesse steeped up closer to the fire, held his hands out toward the flames, and said, "Whew, that fire feels good."

The shadows began to disappear as the early light of dawn chased them away. The fog, too; I could see the bank on the other side of the creek.

"I shore is hungry," Poudlum said while he tossed more wood on the fire. "Anybody else?"

"I'm so hungry I could eat a goat, hair, hide, horns and all," Frank answered. "It's a shame we went and ate up all that fish last night. Some of it shore would go good this morning."

Hunger pangs were stabbing away at me too, and I was just about to pull the store-bought stuff out of my sack when Poudlum said, "We might be able to have us some mo' fried fish."

Almost salivating, Frank said, "How you gonna do that, boy? You gonna be Jesus and just reach in your sack and pull out some fried catfish filets?"

I knew what Poudlum was talking about. It was the trot line. If we had fish on it, then we could have ourselves a hot breakfast.

"Come on, Poudlum," I said as I began removing my shoes and socks. "I'll wade over and untie the other end and drag it across the shoals. You just hang onto this end and help me pull it in.

"Y'all want to help us, Mister Jesse, Mister Frank?"

"We'll help," Frank said, "You think you got any fish on that line?"

"We might have. If we do, I need you to take 'em off the hook and knock 'em in the head so they won't flop around and get back into the water."

I rolled up the legs of my britches and stuck my foot into the water. It was so cold it hurt. I jerked it back out real quick. Poudlum and Frank were standing there waiting on me so there was nothing to do except plunge into the icy water. I gritted my teeth and began splashing across the shoal, and with water sometimes up to my knees, I had forgotten about the cold by the time I got to the other side of the creek.

I whipped out my pocketknife and cut the cord loose from where I had secured it late yesterday. With three loops of the cord wrapped around my wrist I began the journey back across the creek.

About halfway there I began to notice the weight and pull of the cord as it cut into my wrist. I slowed down, searched for firmer footing and continued my trek back across the cold water. After several more steps the line got even heavier and I slipped on the slick surface beneath the water. I went down to my knees and the shock of the cold water up to my waist almost took my breath away.

When I attempted to regain my footing I lost ground and slipped down to the very edge of the rocky shoal just before it dropped off into the deep, dark and cold water below.

Poudlum saw my plight and shouted from the far shore, "Turn it loose! Let de line go!"

I just couldn't because I could tell there was a pile of fish on our trot line.

Another slip and I was down on my belly in the cold water. My feet and legs were swept over first while I clung to the edge of the rocky ledge by my fingernails. Just before I was swept off into the deep water I felt two strong hands grab my shoulders.

I looked up and saw Jesse. "I gotcha, boy, hold onto that line!" He drug me back to my feet on the shoal and helped me walk all the way back to our side of the bank. When we got there I was wet, cold and shivering, but I knew I was safe.

Poudlum and Frank took the cord off my wrist and pulled the line up on the bank. I lay there shivering, along with several big, fat, flopping catfish.

"You need to get out of them wet clothes," Jesse said. "You got any dry ones?"

I had an extra pair of pants and a sweat shirt in my sack. I quickly shed my wet clothes by the fire and slipped into the dry ones.

"Your lips done turned blue, boy," Jesse said while he handed me my quilt. "Put this around you. You shivering like a dog trying to pass a peach seed."

For a moment I thought I detected real concern in his voice. The next thing he did was hang my wet clothes on some bushes to dry, and he placed our wet shoes and socks next to the fire to dry.

While we were doing all this Poudlum and Frank had been cleaning the fish. They brought the filets over next to us stacked up all clean and wet on the big flat rock.

Poudlum dug out the skillet along with the lard and

cornmeal mixture after he had raked out a hot bed of coals to cook on. Frank took over from there and the fish were soon sizzling away, giving off an aroma that had us all moaning in anticipation.

"Them fish sure do smell better swimming in hot grease than they do in cold water," Frank said as he flipped the filets with my fork.

"How many was on the line?" I asked in a weak, shaky voice.

"Dey wuz six nice big ones," Poudlum said. "Would've been seven, but de turtles got to one of 'em. Nothing left but his head, but from de size or it, de turtle got de biggest one."

Jesse was adding more wood to the fire when he leaned over and asked me, "You warm yet?"

"Yes, sir. I'm warm on the outside and I'll be warm on the inside soon as I eat me a piece of that fish."

"Won't be long now," Frank said as he gave the filets one last turn.

"Instead of them fish being out here by the fire with us, you was almost in the water with them," Jesse said as he reached over and tousled the hair on my head.

Poudlum broke out a fresh brown paper bag and Frank forked our breakfast out of the skillet onto the bag to cool. After he had raked out a new batch of red-hot coals and started the second mess of fish frying, we each helped ourselves to a crunchy slab of the sweet meat.

"What you think?" Frank said, obviously to Jesse.

"Just about the best thing I ever put in my mouth," Jesse replied.

"It don't get no better dan dis," Poudlum said. "Tastes so good cause dey so fresh."

"Yeah, couldn't get no fresher," Frank said as he smacked his greasy lips.

Poudlum and I kept up with the bank robbers. We both ate three filets, just like they did. "I'm so full I'm 'bout to pop," Poudlum said as he stretched out beside the fire.

We all just lounged around the fire for a while after we had devoured half the fish in the Satilfa. The last pretenses of night had faded away and the first warm rays of sunshine crested the tree tops, glinted off the sparkling water of the creek, and flooded over our campsite.

Jesse and Frank got up and stepped into the edge of the woods to take care of their morning toiletries, leaving Poudlum and me a brief opportunity to communicate privately.

"Poudlum," I hissed. "You think we ought to just run for it?"

"Naw," he whispered back. "Dem grown mens could run us down 'fore we got to de road."

"You probably right. And if they didn't catch us they could shoot us with that shotgun."

"Uh uh, I took care of dat big scattergun."

"What you talking about?"

"I took de shells out of it dis morning while everybody wuz still asleep and chunked 'em in de creek."

"I betcha Jesse's got more shells in his pocket."

"Won't do him no good," Poudlum grinned.

"How come?"

"'Cause I put a handful of sand in de breech of de shotgun 'fore I closed it back up."

"He's gonna be mad when he finds that out."

"Better he be mad than us be shot."

"I reckon you right on that, Poudlum. What you think they gonna do with us?"

"I don't know, but I don't think dey gon hurt us."

"What makes you think that?"

"'Cause I think dey likes us. I know Mister Jesse was real worried 'bout you slipping over de shoals into dat deep hole. Dey may be bank robbers, but I don't think dey gots it in 'em to harm us."

"You remember that riddle Frank said about the money just before we went to sleep last night?"

"I shore do," Poudlum said. "I said it over and over in my head so I wouldn't forget, 'cause dat's how we gon find de money. We just gotta solve dat riddle."

"We need us some kind of a plan for right now though. We can't just keep sitting around here on the creek bank eating catfish with two bank robbers."

"Well, I can't think of no plan right now except to just play along. If we do dat, maybe we'll get lucky somewhere along de way."

"Are you saying no plan is the best plan?"

"Something like dat, I reckon."

"Shhh, here they come," I cautioned.

"What you boys talking about?" Jesse asked as he stepped back up next to the fire.

Poudlum didn't miss a beat. "We just discussing fish bait, Mister Jesse."

"Huh?"

"Yes, sir, we trying to decide if dem fish gon go for some more sawyers, or if dey gon bite better if we use earthworms and grasshoppers."

"Don't y'all never get tired of fishing?" Frank asked.

"Dis is probably de last chance we gon get to fish till springtime next year. Real cold weather be here 'fore you know it, and we be making syrup and going to a hog killing, so we just be trying to get our fill of it, enough to last us till next year."

Jesse took his hat off, scratched his head and looked off into the distance, signed and said, "You know, boys, I sure do envy y'all for the joy you derive from being out here in the woods living off the land without a care in the world." He continued, "I also admire your honesty, your innocence, and most of all your manners, you know, your respect and your politeness. Y'all can both tell your mommas they ought to be proud of you."

Poudlum and I had that look between us again, and I knew he was thinking like me, that Jesse wouldn't have such kind words for us if he knew we had jimmied his shotgun and planned to escape at our first opportunity.

But our feelings changed immediately as soon as we heard Jesse say, "In spite of all that, the present circumstances have forced us to make a decision. Here's what we gonna do with you boys."

Chapter Seven

ESCAPE

The bridge over the Satilfa Creek on Center Point Road was called the Iron Bridge. That was because the wooden one had been replaced by the current one in 1937, before World War Two began, and it had two steel beams that crossed the creek along with steel railings on each side.

However, the bridge still consisted of mostly heavy lumber. Six-by-twelve pieces of hardwood lumber were bolted to the steel beams all the way across the stream.

Other than the Cypress Hole, the big pool underneath the bridge was the best fishing hole on the creek, that is until you got all the way down to the mouth of the Satilfa where it emptied into the Tombigbee River. Now there was a place where giant catfish abounded! But that was too far from home for us to venture without a grown-up accompanying us.

My daddy would go noodling at the mouth of the creek. That was when he would wade along where the edge of the banks projected out over the water and reach up under them

ESCAPE 71

and yank out big monster catfish with his hands.

A lot of folks who fished under the Iron Bridge threw ropes up and looped them around the ends of the wooden beams and then tied the other end to their boat so they wouldn't drift off downstream while they fished.

Usually, when they quit fishing they couldn't get the ropes loose from the beams above so they would just cut them loose from their boats and leave; consequently, there was an assortment of ropes hanging over the water along each side of the bridge like curtains shielding some kind of mystery under it.

That's where the bank robbers intended to leave us. Frank was up on the bridge cutting loose two of the ropes, which he tossed down to the waiting hands of Jesse on the bank of the creek below the bridge.

"Y'all get on up under the bridge," Jesse ordered us while Frank scrambled back down toward us.

"I hate leaving you boys here," Jesse continued. "But y'all will be all right up under here. Being the resourceful young fellers you are, y'all will figure out something, but it'll be after me and Frank are long gone."

Frank tied us up real tight with the rope he had cut loose while Jesse rummaged through our sacks of supplies.

"I'm going to have to relieve you boys of these biscuits. Please convey our appreciation to your mommas. And some of these canned goods, too."

"Hey!" I exclaimed as he helped himself to our food. "I paid good money for that stuff at Miss Lena's Store."

My eyes bugged out and Poudlum said, "Good Lawd Almighty," when Jesse pulled a big wad of greenbacks out of his pocket and dropped them into my supply sack.

"That'll more than take care of it, boys," he said with a grin.

I was mightily distressed with what they did next. They each reached up and grasped the end of a dangling rope and secured it to the one our wrists were tied with.

"We're sorry to leave you boys like this," Jesse said. "It's just that we need a little time so we can put some distance between us and the sheriff."

"You don't have to worry about us, Mister Jesse," Poudlum said. "We don't have no truck wid dat sheriff."

"I don't doubt that, son," Jesse said as he checked the knots on the ropes. "But they'll make y'all tell the truth, and we wouldn't want you to lie anyway. Ain't that right, Frank?"

"Sure is," Frank agreed. "And we sure enjoyed camping out with you boys. Best fish I ever had. And don't y'all worry none, 'cause some of your folks will come looking for you when you don't show up at home."

"Uh, Frank," Jesse said, "just one other thing. Relieve the boys of their pocket knives before we go."

I truly believe the bank robbers hated to leave us there under the bridge, but they did. Poudlum and I stood helplessly as they scrambled up the bank toward the road.

The water under the bridge sounded different than it did at the Cypress Hole. There were no shoals or rushing or gurgling water over and around rocks. It was just a steady, low hissing of deep running water, like our very lives were flowing away down toward the Tombigbee.

There was enough slack in the ropes to allow us to sit

down. We just sat there beside the running water in a stunned silence for a little while.

Poudlum broke the silence when he said, "I bet dey is some big snakes up under dis bridge. I don't want nothing to do wid no snake, 'specially wid my hands all tied up."

Because of the length of the ropes up to the bridge we could only retreat about two feet from the water's edge. The creek bank in front of us slanted off steeply straight down into the deep and ominous appearing water.

Poudlum had barely gotten the word "snake" out of his mouth when the head of a big, fat cottonmouth moccasin peeked up out of the water just below our feet.

"Oh, Lawd, you see him?" Poudlum cried out as he swiftly drew his feet up underneath himself.

"Yeah, I see him. Just be real still," I told him in as calm a voice as I could muster.

The snake was moving slow. I knew it was because he was cold-blooded and it wasn't long before he would eat up a bunch of fish and crawl into a hole somewhere and hibernate for the winter. The snake was looking for his last meal of tasty fish, just like we had been doing.

I hoped it would swim on down the creek, but to our horror it slowly slithered onto the bank and coiled up in a narrow beam of sunlight coming through a crack in the boards above, just a few feet from us.

"Just be perfectly still," I whispered to Poudlum.

"I don't know if I can," he whispered back.

"You got to. Maybe he'll crawl off in little bit." I reassured Poudlum, but I knew that snake had found itself a patch of sunshine and it wasn't going anywhere for a while.

"Yeah, and maybe it'll start crawling toward us till we runs out of rope," Poudlum softly moaned.

It had a pointed head and a fat body as big as one of mine or Poudlum's arms, both signs of being a poisonous viper. I knew, and I knew Poudlum knew, that to be bitten by that snake could be fatal, especially in our current situation.

There was a smooth, round creek-rock about the size of a small watermelon between Poudlum and me. I directed him to it with a nod of my head and my eyes. We judged the distance in our minds and figured we had enough slack in our ropes to accomplish what we had in mind.

We ever so slowly moved our fingertips into the dirt surrounding the rock and gently lifted it out of the soft ground. Together we slowly raised it above our heads.

"Ready?" I whispered.

"Uh-huh, just say when."

"Now!" I cried out. We hurled the rock as hard as we both possibly could directly at the length of coiled black death below our feet.

In the heat of summer the snake may have been swift enough to escape the rock, but the cool weather had made it slow and stiff.

The split second before the impact I saw it raise its lethal head and bare its fangs inside a mouth whiter than unpicked cotton. Its slender, red, forked tongue flickered once before the rock crushed its head.

We simultaneously breathed a huge sigh of relief as the spasms of the dead viper caused the body to flop back into the creek where it disappeared beneath the surface.

"Dat will teach dat snake to mess wid us," Poudlum said with a tone of obvious relief in his voice.

"Yeah," I agreed, breathing hard.

"Now we gots to get loose and get out of here," Poudlum said.

"That wouldn't be a problem if they hadn't taken our pocket knives."

"Let's try to untie each other," Poudlum suggested.

We struggled with the hard knots on each other's wrists until our fingers ached before we gave up, but almost immediately I came up with another idea.

"If we could climb these ropes up to the edge of the bridge we could climb on top and pull the end of our ropes off the beams. We would still have our hands tied, but we would be loose."

"Sure would be," Poudlum agreed.

He looked up toward the bridge and out toward the creek, thinking about it for a few moments before he continued. "But if you got part of the way up and slipped, you would fall in the creek, and you knows I ain't no swimmer."

"All right, I'll go then. If I fall in the creek I'll just swim back over here to the bank and you can pull me out."

"You done been in de creek once today. You sure you wants to chance it again?"

"I'll chance it 'cause it's the only way I can think of to get loose. I believe I can do it."

"How you gon do dat wid yo' hands tied?"

"I'll use my legs along with my hands. I think there's enough slack so I can wrap my legs around the rope to hold me up while I use both hands to pull myself up a ways.

If I alternate using my hands and legs I should be able to make it."

I twisted the rope around my legs, reached as high up it as I could, got a firm grasp with my hands, and told Poudlum, "Here I go!"

As soon as I left the bank the rope carried me out over the water where I began to swing like a pendulum. As I watched the water skim the bottom of my shoes, I became afraid that I had made a mistake. But it was too late to turn back and there was nothing left to do except give it a try.

I pulled myself upward with my hands and arms and it worked. My feet no longer skimmed along the surface of the water. But I was only about one third of the way up when my arms and shoulders began to ache so bad until I felt like I couldn't make another pull.

Poudlum sensed my distress from down below. "Wrap yo' legs around de rope real tight and just rest yo' arms a while," he called up.

I tried it and it worked. With my legs coiled around the rope I just hung in midair for a while until the pain eased off.

I labored at this process until sweat flooded my eyes, burning them and blurring my vision. By twisting my head I found I could wipe the perspiration out of my eyes on the shoulder of my shirt.

I was almost there. Up above I could see the rough texture of the wooden beam my rope was tied to. It was just inches away.

I coiled my legs around the rope for what I hoped was the last time and reached up. Just as my fingertips brushed the rough wood there was a loud pop, like a rifle shot.

At first I thought someone might be shooting at me, but then the frazzled end of the broken rope just appeared before my eyes and suddenly I was descending through the air with nothing to hang onto.

It stung and shocked me when I hit the surface of the water. Then the force of the fall plunged me deep beneath the surface where I fully expected the mate of the big cottonmouth to be waiting for me with open jaws.

Thankfully, I didn't reach the murky bottom and began kicking and pulling upward with my hands toward the surface as soon as the force of my descent slowed.

When I surfaced, spitting and spewing water, I saw Poudlum wading in to pull me out. I knew he couldn't swim, and I was too exhausted to pull him out of the creek.

"Stay back," I called out weakly as I began to dog paddle toward the shore.

About the same time I felt the bottom under my feet, I felt Poudlum dragging me out onto the bank.

"Lawd, dat scared me when you went under. I was afraid you wouldn't come back up. Is you all right?"

"Yeah, I'm okay," I sputtered, laying limp and shivering on the bank.

"Dat wasn't exactly what we had in mind, but it worked. You loose from de bridge," Poudlum said.

For the second time that morning I stripped out of wet pants. The set I had dried by the fire after my dousing while retrieving the trot line was in my sack. I would just have to shiver in my wet shirt until I could somehow get my hands untied.

The money Jesse had dropped into my sack fell out when I drug my clothes out. Poudlum counted it while I shivered in my wet shirt.

"How much is it?" I asked through cold, blue lips.

"Whew, doggie!" Poudlum whooped. "Mr. Jesse done left us forty dollars!"

"Well, that'll more than cover the cost of my sardines, potted meat and crackers they took."

"Yeah, de biscuits too," Poudlum said. "I bet my momma never knew her biscuits were worth five dollars apiece."

"Let's get out from under here, Poudlum. I'll toss your rope down just as soon as I get up there on the bridge," I called out over my shoulder as I scrambled up the bank, dragging my rope behind me.

"Dat sure does suit me," he called out as he stuffed the money in his pocket.

After I loosened the rope that Poudlum was attached to and tossed it down to him, it was only moments before he joined me up on the road. By then I had figured out a way to get our hands untied.

The rails on the Iron Bridge were sharp and rough. We placed the rope on our trussed-up wrists on its edge and sawed back and forth until the knotted ropes were cut through and fell off, and we were finally completely free.

The money was in dollar bills. As Poudlum counted out my half he said, "You think dis is some of de money they robbed from dat bank?"

"I expect it probably is, but after what Jesse and Frank put us through we ought to get something for our troubles as well as for our food."

Poudlum concurred with me as we put our new-found wealth away. We also agreed not to discuss it with anyone else unless it was absolutely necessary.

"How long you think it's been since they tied us up and hightailed it out of here?"

Poudlum held his hand over his eyes to shade them from the morning sun, judged its height in the sky, and said, "I 'spect it's been about two hours. Less time than Mister Jesse thought it would take us to get loose, I bet you on dat."

"Yeah, I think they expected us to be here until folks missed us at home and come looking for us, which would have been sometime tomorrow afternoon."

"And we would've had to sleep under dat bridge without a fire. I'm thinking less of dem bank robbers all de time," Poudlum said.

"Let's sit down here beside the road for a minute, Poudlum. We need to catch our breath and figure out what we need to do."

We settled down on the soft brown grass beside the dirt road and dangled our feet in the ditch.

"Don't you think we ought to be getting on down de road so we can report dem bank robbers?"

"I ain't sure what we ought to do," I told Poudlum.

"Teacher say we ain't supposed to say ain't."

"Yeah, mine says that, too. Who we going to report them to?"

"I don't know. Whoever we sees first, I suppose."

"They got a good two-hour start. They could've done made it to the river and crossed it already. Or, if they caught a ride they could even be in Mississippi by now."

"Dat's true," Poudlum said. "Mister Jesse and Mister Frank, dey smart. Look how dey fooled de sheriff and come up de creek instead of going down it. How we know which way dey went?"

"You're right, Poudlum. They could have gone in any direction after they left us under the bridge. Shoot, they could have even gone back down the creek 'cause they already been looked for down there. You know the sheriff wouldn't be looking for them to do that."

Poudlum began chuckling.

"What you laughing at?"

"I just remembered what you told me yo' daddy said about de sheriff, dat he couldn't catch a rabbit wid a pack of bluetick hounds."

"Uh, huh, but the sheriff will get help hunting the bank robbers."

"What you mean?"

"All them state and federal lawmen join in the hunt when somebody robs a bank. They never get away anymore. They always catch 'em sooner or later."

"So it don't matter if we just goes on back up to de Cypress Hole and finishes our weekend of fishing, like we never knowed nothing about dem bank robbers, since dey gon get caught sooner or later anyway?"

"I don't know. That's what we trying to figure out. Them bank robbers have already ruined the first part of our fishing trip. Why should we let them ruin the rest of it?"

"If we goes running off down de road looking for somebody to tell, den dat's what we'll be doing, ruining de rest of de weekend."

We looked longingly at the mouth of the trail leading to the Cypress Hole, and yearned for the freedom to disappear down it and continue our fishing trip, but we both knew what the right thing to do was.

We had to report what we knew about the bank robbers.

We didn't say anything else, just picked up our gear and began jogging back toward Center Point. But after only a few steps we observed the dust cloud of a vehicle approaching us from down the road.

Chapter Eight

THE HIDEY HOLE

Who you think dat could be?" Poudlum asked as he squinted his eyes down the road toward the approaching dust cloud.

"I don't know, it could be anybody."

"Might be yo' Uncle Curvin. He said he might come back and check on us."

We stood still in the road watching as the cloud of dust increased in size.

"What we gon do, jus' stand here in de road and wait to see who it is?"

"No," I told Poudlum. "I think we better get out of sight in case it's somebody we don't want to talk to."

"Who in de world would we not be wantin' to talk to?"

"It could be the sheriff, and I sure don't want to talk to him."

"How come?"

"I would just feel better if I could talk to Uncle Curvin before I talked to him, wouldn't you?"

"Uh-huh, I think I would now dat you mentions it. We need a grown person we trust to be with us 'fore we tell what happened to us."

Poudlum and I had minds that followed the same logic to reach a conclusion, that flowed in the same direction like creeks and rivers to reach the sea.

"That's exactly what I think, Poudlum. Let's move!"

The dust cloud grew larger and the approaching vehicle was just moments from rounding the bend, which would put us and the bridge in clear view of whoever occupied it.

"Come on!" I encouraged Poudlum as we grabbed our sacks and dived over the lip of the bank leading back down to the creek.

We slid, tumbled, and crawled until we were back to the curtain of ropes that hung down from the side of the bridge.

"I don't want to go back under dat bridge," Poudlum said, breathing hard.

"We got to," I told him as I pulled him along, back into the dimness under the Iron Bridge, and sat there huddled on the creek bank as the vehicle above us began to rumble across it.

"Couldn't be Mister Curvin 'cause he would've turned off the road fo' he got to the bridge."

"Yeah, but whoever it is has crossed the bridge now and we won't have to—"

I stopped in mid-sentence when we heard the tires of the vehicle grind to a stop on the gravel just after it had crossed the bridge.

"Dey stopped!" Poudlum whispered as his eyes grew to the size of those of a startled doe.

"Yeah, I heard! Be quiet!"

"Why you reckon de did dat?" His voice hissed across the water.

"I don't know! Hush!"

Someone from up above was saying something. "Back up, I think I saw something on that bridge," a gruff voice said.

The boards of the bridge creaked again as the vehicle backed onto the center of the bridge and came to a halt. The engine went dead and a moment later the silence was broken by the sound of two car doors slamming, one after the other.

"Look at this," the same voice said from up on the bridge.

Poudlum and I looked at each other and nodded, because we both recognized the voice of Sheriff Crowe. We had both dealt with him before. Back in the summer he had hounded Poudlum and his family when he was looking for an escaped black convict. I supposed he had done that because they were the only black folks who lived around Center Point.

The escaped convict had worked and lived at the sawmill before it was dismantled and taken away. His name was Jake.

Jake had been a real friend to both of us, a gentle sage whose only crime had been stealing food and taking it to poor, starving folks, kind of like Robin Hood.

Between him, Poudlum and me, we had exposed a

bootlegger and made off with his ill-gotten gains, which we had used to help our families and to get Jake across the Tombigbee and gone for good.

Now, while we gazed upward and strained our ears, we heard the dreaded voice of the sheriff say to his deputy. "Look at this, here's two hunks of knotted rope just laying here on the bridge. Where do you suppose they come from?"

"Could have fell off someone's truck," the deputy answered.

"I don't think so. They look freshly used too. See how the ends are all frazzled, like somebody sawed them in two or something."

"You want me to have a look around?" the deputy asked.

Poudlum whispered very softly, "Should have tossed dem knotted ropes in de creek."

I nodded in agreement just before the sheriff answered the deputy's question.

"We probably ought to look around a little. Maybe down there underneath the bridge. Why don't you climb on down there and see what you can see?"

"You want me to climb down there and look under this bridge?" the deputy asked in an incredulous tone.

"That's what I said," the sheriff answered.

"But it's real snaky down there, and besides, I got me on a clean uniform."

"Do like you told, or you won't be wearing a uniform at all," the sheriff threatened. "I'll look off the other side of the bridge and see if I see anything down the creek."

Poudlum gripped my arm hard and said with a stammered whisper, "We—we—we trapped down under here!"

The sounds of the deputy gingerly picking his way down the bank drifted towards us, and I knew I had to make a decision, so I did.

I leaned close to Poudlum's ear and whispered, "It's all right, I know a hiding place."

My brother Fred had discovered it and shown it to me. And at the time he had made me promise not to ever reveal it to another living soul. But I knew he would release me from that promise if he knew the situation Poudlum and I were in.

When the old bridge had been replaced with the new Iron Bridge, some of the beams of the old bridge had tumbled halfway down the bank under the bridge and had been abandoned there. The beams were solid heart-of-pine, almost as hard as stone and would probably turn into petrified wood eventually.

The unique thing was that they had fallen together to form a bunker, which was hidden when you climbed up into it. No weeds or anything grew inside because the abutment of the new bridge blocked the sunlight from reaching it.

When we quietly scampered inside of it, Poudlum cast his eyes about and whispered, "Dis is some kind of neat place. It's high up above de creek and under the edge of de bottom of de bridge where can't nobody see you."

"Shhh," I cautioned as the deputy came crashing underneath the bridge.

"See anything?" the sheriff called down from above.

"I see the creek," he sarcastically yelled back.

From above him Poudlum and I eased our heads up over the edge of the top beam and peeked down from our hiding place and watched as he poked around. We watched as he cupped his hand to his mouth and yelled up to the sheriff, "I don't see nothing down here, sheriff."

"All right," the sheriff answered. "Come on back up."

We sat still and quiet for awhile until we heard the car doors slam, the engine start and then the fading sound of the car as it headed on up the road.

"Dey gone!" Poudlum said as he exhaled a long breath.

"Yeah, that was a close one."

"I likes dis place," Poudlum said as he explored around inside the secret hiding place.

"I thought you didn't like being under the bridge."

"I don't, but I do like to be in a safe place when danger is around, 'specially if it's a neat place like dis. We could camp out in here."

"Well, you can't never tell anybody about it because it's supposed to be a secret."

"Who found it?"

"Fred found it and made me cross my heart and promise not to ever show it to anybody."

"He knows I wouldn't tell," Poudlum said. "Besides, I figure he would've done de same thing if he had been in yo' shoes."

"Yeah, that's what I thought too. Let's get back up on the road."

When we were back up on Center Point Road, we were once again undecided about what to do.

"We could still just go back and finish our fishing weekend like we never had no visitors," Poudlum said.

"We can't fish any more. They took our knives, remember?"

"Dat's right, we couldn't clean no fish even if we caught
some."

"We could just camp out and not fish, but those greedy
bank robbers only left us enough to eat for tonight. We
would be starving in the morning."

"All right," Poudlum agreed. "Let's head toward home.
We can be there before dinner time."

The only sound besides our footsteps in the dirt was
the rustling of the last few leaves as they fell from the oaks,
hickories, and other hardwood trees along the road. An
occasional green area appeared where there was a patch of
pines or cedar trees.

"What y'all been studying in school?" Poudlum asked.

"We been learning all kinds of stuff. Math, science, his-
tory, literature, and stuff like that."

"Us too. What yo' favorite one is?"

"I don't really like any of them, but if I had to pick one
out I guess it would have to be the literature. It's fun to read
some of the stuff. How about y'all?"

"We doing about de same stuff," Poudlum said. "But,
you know, it seems like to me it would make a lot mo sense
if we all did it in the same school 'stead of separate ones,
don't you think?"

I wasn't sure how to answer Poudlum, so I just agreed
with him and kept on walking. But I resolved myself to
ponder the real answer to his question.

The Center Point Road Baptist Church came into view as we rounded the curve.

"Dere's yo' church up ahead," Poudlum.

"Yeah, that's where I usually spend every Sunday morning, no matter what."

"Any of yo' family buried in that graveyard next to it?"

There was a large cemetery on the left side of the church. "Yeah, I got a lot of uncles, aunts, cousins, and grandparents buried in it. You know how many dead people are buried in it?"

"How many?"

"All of 'em," I told him.

We laughed together and had almost passed the cemetery when I had a thought. "Poudlum, my granddaddy wrote a poem about dying and it's on his tombstone. You want to let's go read it?"

"Uh-huh. Long as it's daylight. I'll go in a cemetery, but you ain't gonna catch me in one after dark."

"Come on then," I told him. "You'll like it."

There was a fence around the graveyard, but the gate was never locked. Folks liked to bring in flowers on special occasions and put them on tombstones.

On this occasion, someone had left a bundle of wild purple violets on my granddaddy's grave.

We stood in front of his big tombstone and Poudlum read the poem out loud:

Where has my youth flown to
On the relentless wings of time
It left me abruptly and without warning

Taking with it the sweet taste of wine
The wind-filled sails seemed so slow
Yet they raced across the decades
Until the wonderful ports of call
All became memories within my gaze
Only yesterday I was a young soldier
Fearing no evil or the shadow of death
And the winds of war left me still alive
But the winds of time have given me no rest
Though the blustery winds have blown me far
From the endless journey I once imagined
At last they took me to a valley of green and gold
Where I shall begin again and never grow old

"Dat's a beautiful poem," Poudlum said. "Was he yo' momma's daddy or yo' daddy's daddy?"

"My momma's. We called him Pa Will. His name was William Murphy. His daddy was Jim Murphy and Jim's daddy was Tim Murphy, who came over here all the way from Ireland in 1821."

"Good Lawd," Poudlum exclaimed. "Dat was way over a hundred years ago. I 'spect my great-great-granddaddy was still chained up then."

"What you mean, chained up?"

"All us colored folks be slaves back den."

"Yeah, I forgot about that. But y'all ain't slaves no more, Poudlum."

"It's true don't nobody own us no more, but you and me, we still can't do a lot of things together."

As far as I was concerned, I would have loved to have

shared a school classroom with Poudlum. Even though we were different, we were a lot alike. We were both the youngest child in our respective families and we would both be twelve years old this month. My birthday was the seventeenth and his was the sixteenth, making him one day older than me, a fact about which he never ceased to remind me.

I had been called a "nigger lover" because of our friendship, but that didn't bother me.

As we were closing the gate to the cemetery, Uncle Curvin's old truck came skidding up to a halt next to the fence.

He leaned out the window and said, "I was on my way to the Cypress Hole when I seen you boys up here. Looks like y'all done cut your fishing trip short."

While we were loading our sacks on the back of the truck, Poudlum leaned over and whispered, "We got to be careful 'bout what we say to anybody."

"What you mean?" I asked.

"We don't want to mention dat riddle Frank told us, 'cause I think dem bank robbers left all dat money somewhere back yonder in de Satilfa Creek."

CHAPTER NINE

CHEWING SUGARCANE

We lost our knives so it was no use to catch no more fish 'cause we wouldn't have been able to clean them," I told my uncle. It wasn't really a lie, we had lost our knives, and that was one of the reasons we hadn't continued with our fishing trip.

"Well, did y'all catch any before you lost your knives?"

"Yes, sir," Poudlum blurted out. "We caught over a dozen big cats and a few nice perch, too."

"Doggone, boys, it sounds to me like y'all had some good luck. What did you use for bait?"

"Mostly sawyers," Poudlum answered.

"They do make good bait," Uncle Curvin said. "But the best bait of all is catalpa worms. Only thing is, they don't make theyselves available 'cept for 'bout two weeks every summer. I'll keep a watch out and when they show up on the trees next summer, I'll take you boys over to Horse Shoe Lake and we'll catch a passel of fish. What did y'all do with all them fish? You couldn't have ate all of 'em."

"We had some of 'em for supper last night and some

more of 'em for breakfast dis morning, and dey wuz mighty good," Poudlum told my uncle.

"I 'spect they was, but what about the rest of 'em?"

Poudlum look in my direction, asking for help with his eyes. That's when I knew I was going to have to tell my uncle a fish story. "We had 'em on a stringer and let 'em go after we lost our knives."

Lies compound themselves and lead to more lies, beginning with the first one.

"How in the world did both of y'all come to lose your knives?"

I decided to tell my fib and leave Poudlum to make up his own. "I lost mine in the creek when I slipped down on the shoals while I was running the trot line."

Nobody said anything for a few moments until Poudlum realized I had left him to make up his own story. "Uh, I ain't real sure 'bout mine," he said. "Last I remember using it wuz when we wuz playing mumblety-peg. It must've just slipped outta my pocket somewhere."

After Poudlum finished with his fib, he cut his eyes toward me, and I knew he was asking what I thought of his fish story. It was amazing how Poudlum and I could communicate with each other without even using words. I grinned my approval toward him.

Uncle Curvin was sympathetic about our loss. "Next time I go to Grove Hill, I'll stop by the hardware store and get both you boys a new knife. Y'all save your money and maybe we can afford to get both of you a Barlow. A fellow needs to have a good pocketknife on him."

We were almost to Miss Lena's Store when Uncle Curvin

said, "That sorry old Sheriff Crowe came by Lena's a while before I headed down y'all's way. It looks like them bank robbers got clean away. He said he couldn't find hair nor hide of 'em no matter where he looks. He headed up toward the Satilfa. Y'all didn't pass him on the road, did you?"

"No, sir. We must have been off the road when he came through," I mumbled, comforting myself with the fact that we had actually been off the road.

"Hey," Poudlum said as we pulled off the road at Miss Lena's Store. "Ain't dat yo' brother Fred sitting over 'side de store?"

I gazed out through the windshield, outlined with milky, white edges from age, and saw that it was indeed my brother. "Yeah, that's him." I answered. "What's that he's got leaning against the tree next to him?"

"Looks like he got hisself a few stalks of sugarcane," Poudlum observed.

As I looked closer, I saw that it was indeed several stalks of sugarcane. Sugarcane was a curse and a blessing to the South.

The curse was the terrible labor it took to grow and harvest it. The plant grew in stalks with joints in each of them like bamboo, except it was solid instead of hollow inside, filled with a thick pulp packed with sweet juice, but encased with a thick and tough peeling on the outside. The stalks were covered with long, slender leaves with edges like a saw blade that would cut your skin and sting for a long time afterward. Planting it and weeding it while it grew was very hard work, and cutting it and harvesting it was even more brutal labor. Back before the slaves were freed, being a worker on a sugarcane plantation was the worst possible place to be.

The blessing of it was that the thick, heavy syrup produced from it was life-sustaining through the winter, and the sugar refined from it was a staple which could be traded for other goods and services.

In 1948, there were no plantations left and certainly no slaves. But folks still grew small patches of sugarcane and made syrup from it. And young boys like us peeled it with our pocket knives and chewed hunks of it for the sweet juice, before we spat out the dry, white pulp.

That's what my brother was doing, chewing sugarcane.

"Y'all must not have caught any fish," he said when we piled out of Uncle Curvin's truck next to him.

He had a big, thick stalk between his legs that he was peeling and chewing. His mouth was full while he talked and there was a pile of dry, spent pulp next to him on the ground that he had chewed the juice out of and spit out.

"Naw, we caught a bunch of fish," I told him. "Where'd you get all that sugarcane?"

"Uncle Clyde gave it to me for helping him cut his. Y'all come on over and chew some. I got plenty."

Uncle Curvin limped into the store to gossip with Lena while Poudlum and I sat down next to the big water oak tree with my brother and each took us a stalk of sugarcane.

After all the slender leaves were stripped from a stalk of sugarcane it was deep blue, almost purple on the outside with a light, silvery transparent film on it. The girth of the stalk increased in size from the top toward the bottom, where it was cut down just above where it emerged from the ground with a sharp machete. The juice got sweeter, too, as you got closer to the bottom of the stalk.

To chew it you had to peel it. To peel it you needed a sharp knife to cut the first joint off, then cut through the tough peeling just above the next joint below that one. Next, you slid the blade of the knife under the peel at the top and pushed it downward to remove the peeling in strips until you had a joint of the stalk reduced to the white pulp.

Now you had to cut off round blocks of this pulp about an inch long, split the block into four parts so it was small enough to put into your mouth, and chew the delectable juice from it before you spat out the dry pulp.

It took a lot of work, but it was worth it. I had tasted a lot of juices, and sugarcane juice was about the best I had ever put in my mouth. I could hardly wait until syrup-making time when we could drink it by the dipper straight from the pulping mill.

"Can I borrow your knife?" I asked my brother.

He had just split enough blocks to last him for a while. As he surrendered his knife he asked, "What happened to yours?"

"I lost it," I told him as I began working on my stalk of sugarcane.

"Where did you lose it?"

"At the creek. All right if Poudlum uses it next?"

"He lose his, too?"

"Yep," I said as I sliced peeling off the stalk.

"Yeah, he can use it too," Fred said. "I just don't see how both of y'all could lose your knives at the same time. And

I've never known of you two to get tired of fishing. I think something fishy is going on." Sometimes I wished my brother wasn't quite as smart as he was.

We chewed in silence for a while, relishing the sweet nectar we hadn't tasted since last year.

Suddenly Fred said, "Did Uncle Curvin tell y'all Sheriff Crowe and one of his deputies came by here heading up Center Point Road toward where y'all was?"

That's when Poudlum let the cat out of the bag. "We seen 'em both and dey would have seen us if we hadn't of hid in yo' hidey hole up under de —"

Realizing what he had done, Poudlum cut his words off.

Fred sat up straight and glared at me. "You broke a promise! Why'd you do that?"

I knew then there was no way out of it. We had to take my brother into our confidence and tell him everything, otherwise he would never understand or forgive me for breaking my promise.

A promise is a promise and should never be broken unless extreme circumstances absolutely force you to. And even then, an explanation should always be forthcoming.

"I had to!" I told my brother. "You would've done the same thing. We had some visitors while we were camping at the Cypress Hole!"

My brother sat up real straight, and I knew I had his attention. "Who? What kind of visitors? What you talking about?"

"I'm talking about the bank robbers, that's who!"

"Uh-uh! How you know it was them? How could y'all even know about the bank robbery?"

"Just hang on, you ask more questions than a school teacher. Uncle Curvin told us about the robbery when we saw him on the road yesterday just before we got to the Cypress Hole."

"Yeah," Poudlum added. "Dey had dat big old scattergun wid 'em dat yo' uncle say dey used to rob de bank!"

Some folks came driving up to the store about that time. "Y'all grab your cane and let's go over to our hideout so nobody will hear what we saying," my brother instructed us.

Our hideout was across Center Point Road and at the back of Uncle Curvin's empty and depleted cotton field. We climbed the fence and made our way between the rows where we had labored under the hot sun back in the summer.

Fred took our cane and carried it for us since Poudlum and I still had our sacks containing our camping gear and food.

The hideout loomed up ahead, gray, weathered, and sagging, with an old rusted tin roof. It was my uncle's cotton house, where the loose cotton had been stored before he hauled it to the cotton gin. It was empty now except for a few field mice that always scurried out when we came in.

This was the place I had helped Jake, the escaped convict, hide out before Poudlum and I helped him float down the Satilfa and across the Tombigbee River on his way to freedom.

We had placed three boards across two of the bare rafters above our heads, and we hid our stuff on top of them so it would be invisible from below.

I sat on Fred's shoulders while Poudlum passed up the canned goods the bank robbers had left us and placed them on top of the boards while we told Fred the story of our encounter with Frank and Jesse.

The only part we left out was the riddle Frank had recited when Poudlum asked them what they had done with the money. When we came to that part of the story, we used our eyes to communicate again. It was spooky, just by the way we looked at each other, we knew that we both wanted to keep that just between us.

When we got to the part where they had told us their names, Fred interrupted us by breaking into uncontrolled laughter. He rolled on the floor of the cotton house with glee.

Poudlum looked at me and said, "What you 'spect so funny to yo' brother?"

I didn't know, but soon Fred stopped laughing and said, "Don't y'all get it?"

"Get what?" I had no idea what he was talking about.

"That wasn't their real names! They were just joshing' y'all like they were the famous bank robbers Jesse James and his brother Frank James."

"Oh," I said. "I never thought about that."

"Don't mean dey names couldn't have really been Jesse and Frank," Poudlum said.

"Not likely," Fred said. "I'm surprised y'all didn't bring 'em here to our hideout," he added with a sarcastic tone.

"We weren't offered the opportunity to bring them anywhere," I told him. "If you remember, they left us tied up under the bridge."

"Oh, yeah," he said. "That was right before they took y'all's pocket knives."

"Dey paid us though," Poudlum said. "Remember. Dey give us each twenty dollars fo' dey lit out."

"Your knives weren't worth anywhere near that. I think they felt bad about leaving y'all and wanted to do something to make up for it," Fred said.

"They owed us for more than the knives," I told him. "We fed them and they took a lot of our food with them."

"Still wasn't worth forty dollars," Fred said. "But I suppose y'all earned it, 'cause I know you both was plenty scared."

"Naw, I wuddn't never too scared," Poudlum said. "Mister Jesse and Mister Frank just seemed like two hungry fellers on de run. And anybody dat likes fried fish as much as dem couldn't be all bad."

"Plus," I told Fred, "we knew they couldn't shoot us."

"How come?"

"I forgot to tell you that Poudlum swiped the shells out of that double-barreled shotgun and put some dirt in the breech while he was doing it."

"They gonna be real mad when they find that out," Fred declared.

"Well that's too bad. They shouldn't have left us tied up under the bridge and taken our knives. We would've just stayed there by the Cypress Hole for a while if they had asked us to."

"Did y'all see any of the money they stole from the bank?"

"We didn't see none of it," Poudlum replied. "Dat is, 'cept de forty dollars dey give us."

"Well, they probably didn't stay on Center Point Road or the sheriff would've caught 'em before coming up on y'all at the bridge. Which way you and Poudlum think they went?"

"I ain't got no idea," I told him. "After they left us under the bridge and climbed up on the road I never heard another sound from 'em."

"I bet I know where they went," Fred said.

CHAPTER TEN

SWEET AND STICKY

From the look I got from Poudlum, I could tell he was as astounded as I was that Fred thought he knew where the bank robbers went. But we both knew Fred was real smart, so we paid attention to what he had to say.

"I 'spect they crossed over the road after they left y'all hogtied up under the bridge and went down the bank on the other side of the road and headed back down the Satilfa toward the Tombigbee."

"Why you think dey woulda done something like dat?" Poudlum asked.

"Because everybody done searched down that way and give up, that's why."

It turned out that Fred's guess was a good one. Frank and Jesse crossed the Tombigbee and made it all the way to Mississippi before they were apprehended at the Greyhound Bus Station two days later over in Waynesboro. However, the only money found on them was a few crumpled-up twenty dollar bills totaling up to a little less than two hundred dollars.

The rumor around the county was they had gotten away with over ten thousand dollars. We all knew that was a heap of money.

On Wednesday, following mine and Poudlum's encounter with the bank robbers, Uncle Curvin came by the house with a copy of the *Clarke County Democrat*'s weekly issue. It had a big story right on the front page about the bank robbery.

My brothers and I gathered around the kitchen table and listened to our mother read the story while Uncle Curvin crumbled up a hunk of corn bread into a bowl of black-eyed peas and spooned the contents into his toothless mouth.

According to the newspaper, instead of the infamous James brothers, Jesse and Frank, the robbers turned out to be Lester Malone and Carl Prescott, two unemployed pulpwood workers from over in Choctaw County, and were both incarcerated in the Clarke County Jail up in Grove Hill.

The paper went on to say there was a great deal of speculation about what they had done with the money, and quoted several people who were of the opinion they had somehow evaded the bloodhounds west of the bridge over the Satilfa on Highway 84 just outside of Coffeeville before they crossed the Tombigbee River and headed toward Mississippi where they were eventually captured.

Fred and I exchanged knowing glances because we knew that no one besides us and Poudlum knew they had actually traveled east on the creek all the way up to the Iron Bridge on Center Point Road and the Cypress Hole before doubling back.

The only thing that took everybody's mind off the bank robbery and the missing money was the coming weekend, which was scheduled for syrup-making, a special and exciting time for everyone except the mule who turned the cane mill.

The pulping of the sugarcane took place a little ways from Poudlum's house where his daddy, Ray Robinson, had a cane mill.

He would hook his mule up to a long pole attached to its collar. The other end of the pole was attached to the top of a contraption with steel rollers set in a wooden frame. While the mule walked in endless circles, folks would feed cane stalks into the roller which squeezed the juices from them.

The juice would come trickling out of a spout from the rollers into a bucket beneath the spout. There was a gourd dipper hanging on the wooden frame, and the best part of syrup-making was that you could step up to the mill, take the dipper, catch yourself some cane juice in it directly from the spout, and drink the sweet, milky juice down without ever having to chew the pulp.

Sometimes you could get a bodacious bellyache from doing that, but the wonderful taste of the juice was worth taking the chance.

Mine and Poudlum's job was to catch the pressed stalks as they came out of the other side of the rollers, crushed and shattered, and pile them aside while making sure the mule didn't step on our feet as we darted in and out of its continuous circulation of the mill.

"Y'all better quit drinking so much of dat juice," Poudlum's mother cautioned us. "Or both y'all be getting' a bel-lyache before you knows it."

The morning mist burned away and it became a clear and cool day, perfect for syrup-making. After the juice was squeezed from the stalks of cane it was transferred to the syrup pans where a hot fire was cooking it. A special aroma filled the air. It was warm and sweet with the promise of syrup and biscuits on all the cold mornings to come.

The only thing I didn't like about syrup making was the stickiness. It seemed to permeate the air and your hands got sticky even without touching anything. I took time to wash my hands every so often to get rid of the feel.

After many hard hours of work, just before it got dark, the finished product was poured into shiny tin buckets and the lids were tapped shut with a rubber hammer.

Uncle Curvin declared it was "sopping good" as the last bucket was sealed.

While the grown-ups were splitting up everybody's share I heard them discussing the bank robbery. "I heard dem bank robbers ain't telling nobody where de money is," Mr. Robinson said.

My Uncle Clyde said, "Do you suppose they just plan to serve their time and then go back and get it?"

"Naw, I don't think so," Uncle Curvin said. "I think they might have give that money to somebody who plans to help them escape from prison."

Everybody had a different opinion, but the one thing on everybody's mind was the money.

"Then again, they could've hid it somewhere between where they left their car there at the Highway 84 Bridge on the Satilfa and the Tombigbee," Uncle Curvin surmised.

"Yeah, but dat's several miles of creek before you gets to de river. Dat would take a lot of looking," Mr. Robinson said as he stacked buckets of syrup on the back of Uncle Curvin's truck.

"Yeah, but still it wouldn't be a bad idea to go down the creek looking for it. Even a blind hog finds an acorn now and again," Uncle Curvin said.

He continued, "I was up in Grove Hill yesterday and the bank has posted a five hundred dollar reward for finding and returning the money."

Poudlum and I were sitting there sharpening our new Barlow pocket knives Uncle Curvin had brought us back from town. "You hear dat?" Poudlum whispered. "Five hundred dollars reward for finding dat money! I figures everybody gon be looking on de wrong part of de creek. Has you figured out dat riddle yet?"

"Naw, but I been thinking on it," I told him.

"We needs to plan us another fishing trip next weekend, 'cept dis time we won't be wasting our time fishin' or humorin' bank robbers."

"Yeah," I agreed. "We got enough food stashed in the hideout to last us the weekend so we won't have to fish. But we need to stay out of trouble this week and bring home some good papers from school so they'll let us go. And remember, we ain't supposed to be saying ain't."

"I ain't forgot," Poudlum said.

That night I dreamed about pulling a trot line out of the Cypress Hole and instead of catfish on the hooks it had big rolls of cash money.

I woke up early Sunday morning and just lay there for a while feeling the comfort of my favorite quilt and listening to my two brother's soft snoring. Any other time I would have gotten a feather and tickled their noses, but this morning I had more important things on my mind.

How could something be wet, but still be dry I wondered? And how in the world could anything be deep and still be nearby?

Whatever the answers were, they were the key to where the money was. I knew that and so did Poudlum. The only thing left to do was solve the riddle.

I was still pondering the answer to the riddle while we sat in church. The collar of the starched white shirt my mother had ironed that morning was chafing my neck even before the new preacher started preaching.

I concentrated on remembering the lesson I had been taught in the cotton field during the hot summer when the sun had beaten down on us unmercifully. It was when Poudlum had taught me, through his family's singing, that you could take your mind to a finer place while your body suffered if you just concentrated on the sweet words of a gospel song.

That's when everybody stood and began singing "In the Sweet Bye-And-Bye," and I was surprised at how quickly I captured the mood and forgot about my stiff shirt collar and the dress shoes squeezing my toes together. The song swept over me just as the one had in the cotton field, and pretty soon I captured the mood and in my mind I was floating down streams and drinking Nehis with little rivulets of cool moisture sliding down the slick surface of the bottles.

After awhile I came out of my trance and became aware of the new preacher talking and soon my attention was riveted to his every word. He was preaching on the Gospel of Mark in the New Testament of the Bible. His voice boomed out over the congregation when he said, "Chapter Eighteen says that in His name we can take up serpents, drink poison, and lay hands on the sick to heal them."

I leaned forward and listened even closer when he said, "Now I don't think the Bible meant we can just handle snakes. Any fool knows if you handle a timber rattler or a moccasin, they are pretty sure to bite you. Snakes are creatures with no soul or feeling that just strike out at anything that threatens them, and therefore they represent evil. I think what the Bible really means when it speaks of handling snakes is that we have to confront evil and face it down. We have to handle evil! Now when the good book says we can drink poison in His name without being harmed, I don't think it's talking about drinking strychnine or whiskey to prove your faith, but rather being able to swallow the inequities and disappointments this old life brings us without losing your faith. And now we come to what some call 'the laying on of hands' in His name to cure disease and deformity. Now, some false prophets will talk you into a trance to make you believe this, but their cure is temporary. The true meaning is that care and providing for the infirmities and illnesses of our fellow man is the way we lay our hands on and attempt to heal."

The preacher paused and wiped his brow. A hush fell over the congregation and I knew then that other folks were listening to what he had to say, too. The silence was broken by an "amen" from somewhere toward the back of the church.

I thought I liked what the new preacher preached. What he said made a lot more sense to me than the ranting and raving of the last preacher.

After the closing prayer Addie Brooks struck a chord on the old piano and everybody stood and joined together singing "I Will Overcome."

Red, yellow, and golden leaves were floating down from the oak trees surrounding the church when the congregation spilled outside. A soft fall breeze caressed all the ladies' hairdos as they milled around and gossiped. The preacher moved from person to person and accepted their praise for a well-delivered and enlightening sermon. There was a small element who held back because I figured they weren't too sure about the way he had interpreted the Bible, but they, too, were polite and courteous to our new preacher.

But everyone agreed on one thing—that there was money hidden on the Satilfa and a reward of five hundred dollars was a fortune that someone among us needed to collect.

Fred and I meandered through the crowd and listened to several theories about where the money was hidden. The consensus was that it was hidden somewhere between the Satilfa Creek Bridge on Highway 84 and the Tombigbee River.

My brother grinned, leaned over and whispered into my ear, "But we know better, don't we?"

"Be quiet!" I scolded him.

It would be a long week before we could escape back

to the creek. It began Monday morning when we all got up early to get ready for school. The taste of the fresh syrup poured from a pitcher onto a hunk of fresh butter, stirred together, and then sopped up with hunks from a hot biscuit brightened the early morning routine. My mother and oldest brother Ned checked Fred and me to make sure we were properly dressed for school, and doled out a nickel and a dime, fifteen cents, to each of us for our lunch money.

I had practiced my spelling words by the light of the fireplace last night and was ready to stand the test I knew awaited me.

While we were walking out to Friendship Road to catch the school bus, Fred said, "One more week after this week and we'll be out of school for Christmas, and we won't have to go back until after the first of the year."

My heart soared! I had plumb forgot. In two weeks we would be free to do as we pleased for the next two weeks, and wouldn't have to go back to school until the third day of the new year.

The Bedwell kids caught the bus at the same spot we did, but they were older, like my brother Ned. They gathered together with him while we waited on the bus, talking about whatever folks in the eleventh and twelfth grade of school talked about, leaving Fred and me free to talk in low tones about what we wanted to.

"I can't believe it's gonna be 1949 before we know it," Fred said. "What do you think things will be like fifty years from now?"

My brother came up with some strange questions. "How

in the world would I know that? I guess we'll just have to wait and see," I told him.

"I can't wait that long," he said.

"You got to!" I exclaimed.

"We can write down what we think," he said. "That'll give us something to do while we're out of school."

My brother was off on another tangent. He had already forgotten about playing checkers and the spinning jenny, and now he wanted to start predicting the future.

I knew I had to get his mind off that before he got too involved into it. He was real smart and Poudlum and I might end up having to ask him to help us solve the riddle.

My brother made straight A's in school and didn't seem to spend much time studying, while I had to work hard to get B's. I kept my voice down when I told him, "Hadn't you rather help me and Poudlum—"

"Poudlum and me," he corrected me.

I had to hurry because I spotted the bus coming over the hill. "Hadn't you rather help us find the money?"

He leaned close and said, "Sure I would, but I wasn't sure if y'all wanted me to."

"We do, so forget about predicting the future right now."

"All right," he said. "When do we start?"

I thought about telling him about the riddle, but wondered if I ought to discuss it with Poudlum before I did.

Before I could make up my mind the school bus pulled up and we had to get aboard.

CHAPTER ELEVEN

UP THE CREEK

School lunches were good, especially on Fridays when we had a peanut butter and jelly sandwich along with a bowl of hot vegetable soup and a carton of milk. It was the Friday before we got out of school for the Christmas holidays and I was enjoying my last favorite school lunch for the year.

So far Poudlum and I hadn't been able to convince our mommas to let us go on another fishing adventure, but we still had plenty of time to win them over.

The peanut butter and jelly sandwich was sweet on my tongue and the soup was warm with a rich taste of okra, tomatoes, and other vegetables. I found myself wondering what Poudlum was having for lunch just a mile down the road .

Once when I had asked him about lunches at his school he said, "Yeah, we got 'em just like you says y'all do, but most folks ain't got fifteen cents to pay for 'em."

"What do y'all do for lunch then?" I asked.

"Most of us brings our lunch. My momma fixes all ours

and we brings it to school in a syrup bucket. Me and my brothers and sisters all share it at lunch time."

"What do y'all eat?"

"Mostly biscuits wid some meat in them. Sometimes we has baked sweet taters and sometimes we have a fried egg in our biscuits. On special occasions a piece of pork or fried chicken, but mostly biscuits with a piece of side meat in it."

As I finished my lunch that Friday I began to think about the plan I had come up with. It was to get Uncle Curvin to drop Poudlum and me, and maybe Fred, off at the bridge over the Satilfa on Highway 84 where the bank robbers had abandoned their car and tricked the authorities into believing they had gone west toward the river, when actually they had turned around and gone east and ended up at the Cypress Hole and ruined mine and Poudlum's fishing trip.

Our story would be we were going to fish our way up the creek and end up at the Iron Bridge on Center Point Road, while in reality we would be retracing Jesse and Frank's trail looking for where they had hidden the money.

I had come home from school with all B's and one A on my report card and my momma had said I could go, but not until Sunday afternoon after church.

The first thing I did Saturday morning was walk over to Poudlum's house to tell him the plan and see if Mrs. Robinson would let him go with me.

The Robinsons were scurrying around doing all kind of chores when I walked into their yard. Old Buster, their dog, who wanted to bite me the first time I ever came to

Poudlum's house, trotted out to greet me, wagging his tail. While I was petting him Poudlum spotted me from the front porch.

"Momma!" he called out. "Ted's here!"

The screen door behind him opened and the lovely, full figure of Mrs. Robinson framed the doorway.

"Hey, Mrs. Robinson," I said as I approached the steps leading up to the porch. "How y'all doing?"

Mrs. Robinson liked me. I could tell by the big smile that broke across her face. "Well bless my soul, I does believe you is right, Poudlum. It is Mister Ted. Come on up here on de porch and set a spell wid us. How's yo' momma and 'em?"

"They doing fine, thank you ma'am," I told her as I sat down on the porch swing with Poudlum.

"I came over here to see if you would let Poudlum go fishing with me on the Satilfa Creek after church tomorrow," I told Mrs. Robinson. "I thought we would start down on Highway 84 and fish our way up the creek to Center Point Road and be home Monday afternoon."

Poudlum couldn't sit still. "Yes ma'am, dat's what we wants to do. I could go straight from church tomorrow afternoon," he said while he tugged gently on his mother's hand.

Mrs. Robinson smiled real big, and I sighed with relief when she said, "I suppose dat will be all right, since you brought dat good report card home."

She told me Poudlum had brought home straight A's. "How about you, Mister Ted? You bring home some good grades?" she asked.

"I got one A and the rest Bs," I told her.

She beamed, and said, "Y'all both mighty fine boys. De Lawd blessed us wid both of you."

"Thank you ma'am. Would it be all right if Poudlum walked up the road a piece with me?"

"Dat will be fine. You know it's gon be hog killing time next week if the weather turns cold. Tell yo' momma I be looking forward to seeing her, and we both will get us a nice Christmas ham."

"I'll be sure and tell her, Mrs. Robinson," I said as Poudlum and I headed down the steps.

As soon as we were out of earshot of the house Poudlum asked me, "You figured out dat riddle yet?"

"Naw. You the straight-A student. You figured it out?"

"Naw, me neither. But I 'spect when we gets out on de creek we'll figure it out."

I sure hoped Poudlum was right, but I wasn't real confident as I remembered Frank's whisper: *It's wet but it's dry, it's deep but it's nearby.*

The First Antioch Church of Christ was just outside of Coffeeville, not far from the colored school. Uncle Curvin and I were sitting inside his truck across the road from it Sunday afternoon. We had driven over there after our church got out. I was afraid we would be late and Poudlum would have to wait on us, but the colored folks were still worshiping when we got there.

"What time is it?" I asked Uncle Curvin.

He slipped out his big round watch, flipped the lid of it up and said, "It's half past one o'clock."

"Good Lord!" I exclaimed. "How long do you expect they stay in there?"

"Them colored folks love to preach and sing," he said.

The words were hardly out of his mouth when I heard the church break into song. I figured that was a good sign, that maybe the preacher had quit preaching.

The sound of the old Negro spiritual, "Going Home," with its inspiring lyrics, came floating out towards us:

I'm a goin home
No more fret nor pain
No more stumbling on de way
No more longing for de day
Gwine to roam no more
Morning Star lights the way
Shadows gone at the break of day
I'm just going home
I'm just going home.

Poudlum spotted us as soon as he came out the front door of the church. He waved, then disappeared inside the cab of Mr. Robinson's truck for a few moments. When he reemerged, he had shed his Sunday clothes and was clad in clothes suitable for traveling up the creek. I watched as he hugged his momma, took his gear from the back of their truck and started jogging toward us.

I slid over in the middle of the seat and he climbed into the truck with us. "Y'all been waiting long?" he asked.

"Not too long. What time does y'all's church start?"

"'Bout eleven o'clock, just like all of 'em."

"You mean y'all have to be in there for two and a half hours?"

"Yep, dat's right. Colored folks like to preach and sing," Poudlum replied.

"Told you," Uncle Curvin said as he shifted gears and guided his truck onto the road.

"You heard anymore about dem bank robbers, Mister Curvin?" Poudlum asked.

"As a matter of fact, I did."

He hadn't told me, so I was all ears. "What did you hear?" I asked.

"Well, boys, I didn't just hear something, I saw it."

Now he really had my curiosity up. "Saw what?"

"I saw the bank robbers. Difference was, this time they were handcuffed instead of holding a loaded sawed-off shotgun."

"Did you see 'em at de jail house, Mister Curvin?"

"Naw, I saw them in the courtroom Friday. They got themselves arraigned in Superior Court."

"What in the world does that mean, Uncle Curvin?"

"Arraignment is when you have criminal charges against you and you appear before a Superior Court judge and make a plea," he explained to us.

Still not clear, I asked, "What's a plea?"

"That's when you plead guilty or not guilty to the charges against you. You can plead guilty and go ahead and take your medicine, or you can plead not guilty and have a trial by jury."

"How did Mister J—" Poudlum caught himself and said, "How did dem bank robbers plead?"

"They both pled not guilty. A jury will be called tomorrow and their trial will start on Tuesday."

"You gonna be there?" I asked.

"I got to be there. The state has called me as a witness against them."

A thought suddenly entered my head. "You think me and Poudlum could go up there with you on Tuesday and watch the trial?"

My uncle didn't have an answer right off. I could see he had to think about it for a while as we rode along. Finally, he said, "I don't see no reason why not, since y'all out of school. I don't know of no law that would keep young boys out of a courtroom as spectators. Of course both of you will have to get the okay from your mommas before I'll take you."

We soon reached the bridge. It was just a bridge built of concrete and steel, with no features to make it unique like the Iron Bridge up on Center Point Road.

While we were unloading our stuff off the back of his truck Uncle Curvin began giving us a little lecture: "Y'all probably won't have to worry about snakes with the weather turning cooler, but there could still be some in the water, so watch out. Take them new Barlow's I got for y'all and cut you both a stout stick soon as you get on the creek. And remember, find you a good camping place before dark. Leave yourself enough daylight to pile up enough wood to get through the night. It'll get cold before morning."

I wasn't familiar with this part of the creek. The furthest I had been down it from Center Point Road was at most a mile. Folks said it was a good four miles from Highway 84 up to the Iron Bridge on Center Point Road. That meant three miles of unfamiliar creek to navigate.

Just after we got all our stuff off the truck and my uncle

finished his lecture, another pickup truck pulled off on the other side of the road. Three men piled out of the cab and began unloading a skiff off the back of the truck. When they got it off, they carried it down the bank on their side and launched it into the creek. Two of them got aboard while the third one pushed the bow of the boat into the water and leapt aboard himself at the last moment. We watched them begin to work their paddles and disappear around a bend of the creek going downstream towards the river.

"Looks like somebody else is going fishing," I said.

"Dey didn't have no fishing poles or nothing," Poudlum added.

"Them fellers ain't going fishing," Uncle Curvin informed us. "They searching for the money."

"Dey be barking up de wrong tree looking down dat way," Poudlum muttered.

"What's that, son?" Uncle Curvin asked.

"Uh-uh, I just said I 'spect it's time we got on our way."

"I think you right. Now, boys, if y'all make it up to Center Point Road by around noon tomorrow, I'll be along that way about that time. By then you boys will have had enough of walking and want a ride."

"I imagine you'll probably be right about that, Uncle Curvin, and we'll be much obliged."

We said good-bye to my uncle and I told Poudlum, "Let's hit the woods."

I heard the sound of the old truck fading away in the distance as we entered the shadows surrounding the Satilfa. There close to the bridge the ground was worn smooth from people fishing from the bank and camping out. There were several dark circles of cinders, the remains of campfires.

Poudlum found us two stout hickory saplings, which we trimmed with our new knives before we left the trampled-down area and started up the creek. We hadn't gone far when Poudlum asked, "Which side of de creek you think Jesse and Frank went up?"

I was stumped by his question and had to think on it for a spell. "They were probably in the creek to hide their scent from the dogs when they came along here, 'cause they had already been down the creek before they doubled back up this way."

"Dat still don't tell us which side they went up."

"We know which side they were on when they got to the Cypress Hole. They were on the far side from us."

"Yeah," Poudlum said. "But dat's a long way up de creek."

"Okay, we'll just watch the banks as we go up the creek, and maybe we can spot where they came out. It makes sense they would come out of the water where there was a sandy bank, so we ought to be able to see their tracks since it hasn't rained since they came up this way."

"Sometimes you can't see the far bank clear enough to spot tracks," Poudlum argued.

"You want to let's separate and one of us go up on each side?"

Poudlum considered that for a moment, then said, "Naw, I think it's best if we stay together. What you think?"

"I think we ought to cross the creek and go up the other

side because that's the side they were on when they got to the Cypress Hole."

We found a shallow place not far up the creek, studded with large rocks, so we crossed hopping from rock to rock and didn't even get our feet wet.

"How far we goin' fo' we stops?" Poudlum asked.

"Let's try to go about halfway."

"How we gon know?"

"We'll just guess."

"What we gon look for while we going?"

"I don't know. Maybe just look for anything unusual."

"Everything along dis creek look unusual to me."

"I mean like some piece of trash, an empty tin can, a broken limb or coals from a recent fire, stuff like that."

We walked and walked but didn't see anything except a beautiful stream secluded by an undisturbed forest. I figured it was about five o'clock, with barely an hour of daylight left, when we stopped. I knew it was time because the light filtering through the trees was growing dim.

It was a perfect campsite, on the sandy beach of a sharp curve in the creek covered with dry driftwood, which we quickly stacked into a pile to feed our fire through the night.

We ate sardines and pork and beans directly from the cans, along with saltine crackers, and washed it down with the sweet water from the creek. We burned the cans and the paper in our fire like Jake had taught us at the sawmill.

The soft flowing sound of the creek, the stillness of the woods, the crackle of the fire, and the warmth of my quilt were a potent combination to cause drowsiness.

"You asleep?" Poudlum asked softly.

"Naw, not yet."

"What you thinking 'bout?"

"That riddle," I told him.

"Maybe if we goes to sleep thinking 'bout it, we'll wake up wid de answer."

"I doubt that'll work, Poudlum," I told him in a sleepy voice. "But I can't think of a better idea, so I'll try it."

The stars sparkled like precious stones in the sky, and the water licked softly at the sandy shore while moonlight danced across the surface of the creek. It all soothed me toward a blissful sleep while the riddle lingered in the back of my mind. *It's wet but it's dry, it's deep but it's nearby.*

When I woke up it was with a jolt, with a clarity of mind as sharp as the edge of a well-honed steel blade, and I knew the answer to the riddle! Well, at least to the first part of it!

CHAPTER TWELVE

DEEP SECRET

What the first line of the riddle meant was that the money was underwater and therefore wet; however, it was also in some kind of container which kept the money dry, so it was wet but it was dry. I was sure of it.

It wasn't a revelation, it was just what made sense. It was like being stumped about something, but then in a quiet and serene moment realizing how simple the answer really was.

That was what happened, and I supposed it was the extreme peacefulness, the isolation of where we were, and the soothing murmur of the creek that had given me the clarity of mind to find the answer.

I was wide awake now. The gray tentacles of dawn were slithering through the overhead branches of the trees, and across the glowing embers of our fire I could see the dim outline of Poudlum curled up in his quilt. He was still sound asleep, breathing deeply.

I was anxious to tell him about the riddle, but I knew I had all day to do that, so I let him sleep while I quietly stacked wood on our fire. It wasn't freezing cold, but it was cold. Being so close to the water made it seem even colder. I was shivering, but now the fire was beginning to crackle and roar as I wrapped back up inside my quilt.

It wasn't long before I heard Poudlum stirring. His head popped out from underneath his quilt like a turtle. "Mm-mmmm, dat fire sho do feel good," he said in a gravelly morning voice.

"You sleep good?" I asked him.

"Like a big old tired rock. You?"

"Yeah, me too."

He sat up, gathered his quilt around him, and scrunched up closer to the fire. "It helped dat didn't no bank robbers come sneaking 'cross de creek and tie us up to dey smelly toes."

We grinned at each other across the fire and held our hands closer to the fire to warm them.

"I sho is hungry," Poudlum said.

I dug two big cinnamon rolls, wrapped in wax paper, out of my sack. They cost a dime each at Miss Lena's Store, but they were bigger than a large man's hand and were covered with a creamy white icing. In anticipation last night, I had cut two long, slim sticks and whittled a sharp point on each of them. We unwrapped the rolls, impaled them on the sticks, and warmed them over hot coals.

With sticky hands and faces but full stomachs, we abandoned the warmth of our fire and lay down on our bellies next to the edge of the creek where we sucked up gulps of the cold water, which washed our hands and faces as it quenched our thirst.

When we got back by the fire, once again warm and content inside our quilts, I told Poudlum how the answer to the first part of the riddle had come to me.

"I knew it would, I just knew it would!" he repeated. "How we gon figure out de second part?"

"I don't know," I said. "We'll just keep going up the creek and somehow we'll do it."

"But we ain't got another night for you to sleep on de bank of dis creek and figure it out."

"I know. Maybe we can figure it out by the time we get to the Cypress Hole."

"What if we don't?"

"Be positive, Poudlum, and start thinking!"

We raked sand over our fire, rolled our quilts up, tucked them in our sacks and started up the creek as the early morning sun warmed our way.

Other than raccoons and squirrels, nothing out of the ordinary attracted our attention until we got to the spot where the Mill Creek merged into the Satilfa. It was there that the remains of the illegal moonshine still, which Poudlum had discovered, loomed up in front of us. It was still a foreboding site, but now lacking the evil and fear it had instilled in us when we had secretly observed its actual operation. We had gone on to implicate the lawbreakers and reaped a nice profit from doing so.

A little further up we passed the Fallen Tree Bridge, which was just what the name implied, a huge tree which had fallen across a narrow spot in the creek and could actually be used as a bridge to cross the creek. This was the spot where Poudlum and I had last seen our friend Jake just before we sent him off on a river to freedom. We lingered, remembered it all, then smiled at each other because we knew we had done the right thing.

By noon we were standing underneath the Iron Bridge on Center Point Road.

"What we gon do now?" Poudlum asked. "We ain't seen nothing to lead us to dat money."

It was a discouraging situation, but I wasn't giving up. "Let's just walk on up to the Cypress Hole on this side of the creek where Jesse and Frank were. They came up on this side, and we were on the other side camping out."

"Yeah, let's see where dey were 'fore dey came across de creek and ate up our fried catfish."

It was just a short walk from the bridge up to the Cypress Hole, but I suddenly realized I had never been up that side of the creek, above the bridge and across from our favorite fishing hole. That is except to one spot to tie our trot line to a tree.

We had only gone a few steps when Poudlum picked up the trail Jesse and Frank had left. "Look at dat!" he exclaimed when he came to a sudden halt and held his arm out in front of me.

"What?"

"It's an old trail, but see how de low bushes are still bent and broken?"

Poudlum was right. There it was right in front of us, a beaten-down path which surely the bank robbers had made.

We proceeded carefully along the path while we watched for clues. "Look for anything, Poudlum, something they might have dropped or left behind."

We searched in vain, but nary a clue did we find, and eventually we were across the creek from our former campsite, the end of the trail. We did find a trampled down area where Jesse and Frank must have lain in wait before they had crossed the creek, ate our fish, and held us as prisoners.

"I bet dis is where dey lay around waiting for it to get dark before dey crossed de creek," Poudlum said.

"I 'spect you right, Poudlum. Let's search around on the ground real close."

We got down on our hands and knees and searched, but there was nothing to be found.

"Doggone dem robbers, dey could've left us some kind of clue," Poudlum said.

"Ain't nothing here. I guess they smarter than I thought they were. Come on, let's cross the creek and go on back to the road. Uncle Curvin ought to be coming along before long."

"We just gon give up?"

"Just for the time being. Ain't nothing else left to do."

There was a black gum tree right close to the bank where the creek-crossing was. Black gums liked to grow near water among pine thickets. Birds loved them, too, because in the fall they were covered with berries. Not berries that were good for people to eat, but birds, especially woodpeckers, liked them.

I noticed the dried remains of bleached-out bird droppings on the tree's roots as they spread out from its base. Just before I stepped on the first rock in the creek I saw something else!

Someone had carved an arrow into the trunk of the tree just above the ground. It was pointing straight down toward the deep water of the Cypress Hole below the rocky shoals!

"Hang on, Poudlum!" I cried out. "Look at that," I said, pointing toward the tree trunk.

At first he thought I had spotted a snake, but I quelled his fear when I pointed directly at the arrow again. We both dropped to our knees and began to examine it. "Somebody carved that in the tree!"

"It looks fresh too," Poudlum observed.

We looked at the arrow and then at the deep water it pointed toward, and we knew—*It's deep but it's nearby.*

The money was on the bottom of the creek below the deep, dark water of the Cypress Hole!

The edge of the forest hung over each side of the creek, leaving only a narrow opening from the sun to touch the water for a brief period during the middle of the day. The sun had crested the eastern edge of the forest and hung directly overhead, sending shimmering light dancing across the surface as we stared down toward the depths of the Cypress Hole.

"How you think dey keeping it dry and how dey got it to stay down without it floating up and away?" Poudlum asked.

"I figure they put it in some kind of water-proof container and then tied it to a big rock before they slid it into the water."

We just stood there staring at the water for a few moments. I knew Poudlum had been thinking the same thing

as I had when he said, "How in de world is we ever gon get
it outta dat water? How deep you think it is?"

"I've heard tell it's about twenty feet deep," I told him.

"Dat money might as well be in China," Poudlum said
as he shook his head in disappointment.

"Hey, we figured out where it was, didn't we?"

"Uh-huh, we did dat, but it appears dat knowing where
it is and getting it is two different things."

"We found it and we'll figure out a way to get it out of
the water, Poudlum."

"I bet you couldn't even see down there. Probably some
giant catfish down there that would swallow you like a worm.
Is you gon go down in dat cold, deep water and get it?"

"I might."

"How you gon find it if you can't see down there?"

"I'll feel around on the bottom for it."

"A big catfish would probably bite one of yo' fingers off
while you wuz feeling around."

"Hush, Poudlum. You just trying to get me scared.
What we need is some kind of a big hook, tie it to a rope
and fish it out."

"Well, we ain't got nothin' like dat."

"What you think we ought to do then?" I asked Poudlum.

"I think we ought to leave it alone for de time being."

"What you talking about, Poudlum? We done gone to
all this trouble and now that we found it just walk off and
leave it?"

"We knows where it is, and it ain't going nowhere. I say
we gots to get us some help and come back later."

I knew Poudlum was right. It was too dangerous a thing for just the two of us to attempt to raise the money by ourselves. "I guess you right, Poudlum. We will have to get some help and come back."

"Who we gon get to help us? You knows we have to share de reward if we does."

"It's a lot of money, that reward, enough to share. We'll get my brother Fred to help us. He'll know how to do it."

"I think dat's a right smart idea. Now let's cross de creek and get outta dese woods."

We hadn't walked quite a half mile down Center Point Road before Uncle Curvin pulled up beside us in his truck. "Hey, boys," he greeted us. "Did y'all bring me some fish?"

"Uh—no sir," I told him as we tossed our sacks onto the back of his truck. "I'm afraid the fish wasn't biting."

"Y'all fished all the way up that creek and didn't catch any?"

"We didn't catch nary one fish, Mister Curvin," Poudlum volunteered.

It wasn't really a lie, I thought. Of course we had not tried, but we still didn't catch any fish.

"Well, boys, that's just the way it is," my uncle said. "You never know exactly when the fish are going to bite. If we did we would only go fishing on those occasions. But I do have some good news for y'all."

I couldn't imagine what kind of good news he had for us, but I wanted to know, and I was sure Poudlum did too. We climbed into the cab of the truck, and after it began rolling down the road I asked him, "What kind of good news, Uncle Curvin?"

"I went up to the courthouse in Grove Hill early this morning," he said as he shifted into third gear and released the clutch with his foot. "The trial for the bank robbers is gonna start tomorrow just like I said, and I have to be in court as a witness to testify against them."

"Ain't you scared to do dat, Mister Curvin?" Poudlum asked.

"Why would I be scared, son?"

"What if dem bank robbers ever gets out of jail and come back looking for you for testifying against 'em?"

"Yeah, what if that happens?" I agreed.

"Well now, this is a good lesson in life for you boys. The lesson is that you got to do the right thing and not be afraid of the consequences. If you do right and something bad happens to you, you still know you done right. But chances are that if you do right, you won't have to worry about that and will have peace of mind. On the other hand, if you do wrong, you gonna be worried all the time."

My uncle rambled on a lot, but I realized he was right. I could tell Poudlum did, too, by the way he was nodding his head.

"What you think dey gon do wid dem bank robbers, Mister Curvin?" Poudlum asked.

"In my opinion, I think they'll send them off to prison for quite a spell."

"But they do get a trial to see if that happens, don't they?" I asked.

"Oh yeah, they'll get a trial 'cause in the eyes of the law they're innocent until they're proven guilty."

"But you saw 'em do it!" I exclaimed. "You know they guilty!"

"The wonderful thing about this country, boys, is what I told you about being innocent until you get proved guilty. Over across the ocean, where we all came from, it's just the opposite. Over there you're guilty until you prove yourself innocent."

"You think our way is better?" Poudlum asked.

"Uh-huh, I do, because our way protects the innocent. And guilt or innocent is determined by a jury of twelve citizens, who after hearing all the evidence from both sides, make a decision. And even that decision can be appealed if just cause is shown."

"What's an appeal?" I asked him.

"An appeal means the final decision ain't really final if a lawyer can find a reason to make it seem wrong. You see, boys, the worst thing in the world is for an innocent person to be punished for a deed they didn't do, and in our country every possible effort is taken to see that don't happen."

Riding down a dirt road in an old pickup truck, a crippled old war veteran had taught Poudlum and me something very important that no one had thought to teach us in school so far.

When we passed Center Point Road Baptist Church I said, "Hey, Uncle Curvin, you said you had a surprise for us."

"Oh yes, I do. I've got a good surprise for both of y'all."

CHAPTER THIRTEEN

THE COURTHOUSE

I couldn't imagine what kind of surprise Uncle Curvin had for Poudlum and me. He had already gotten us brand new pocket knives to replace the ones Jesse and Frank took from us. Maybe he was taking us to Miss Lena's Store for a Nehi and a Moon Pie, but no, he would have just said that. It had to be something more special.

"You say the surprise is for both of us, Uncle Curvin?"

"Yep, you and Poudlum both," he said as he grinned his toothless smile.

It was as if he was taking satisfaction in keeping us in suspense while he just kept driving on down the road.

"Well," I told him, "what did you bring it up for if you ain't gonna tell us what your surprise is?"

"All right, all right," he said. "Just keep your britches on. The surprise is that I got everything okayed with both y'all's mommas," Uncle Curvin said with glee.

"What you talking about, Mister Curvin?" Poudlum piped up. "What you got okayed with our mommas?"

We were at the bottom of the hill leading up to Center

Point Road Baptist Church, leaving a cloud of dust behind us. Uncle Curvin depressed the clutch of the old truck and shifted into second gear so it would grind on up the hill. After he did that he said, "Remember how y'all said you would like to go see the trial of the bank robbers?"

"Yes, sir, we remember," I said eagerly.

"Well, I fixed it so y'all can. The judge and the lawyers are selecting the jury today and the trial is going to start in the morning. Done talked to both your mommas about it and got their blessings for y'all to go up to Grove Hill with me and watch the trial."

Poudlum and I looked at each other and sparks flew between our eyes, because we knew we were going to get to see Jesse and Frank again, and this time they would be the ones trussed up so they couldn't escape.

"How in the world did you ever do that, Uncle Curvin?"

"I told 'em it would be good for y'all's education to see how the courts and our justice system works."

"And dey said okay to dat?" Poudlum asked with disbelief.

"Uh-huh, they did, but I believe they did because they had other reasons in mind besides you boys learning something about how our court system works."

"What you mean by that?" I asked.

"I think they both figured you boys would get into less devilment up there with me than you would rambling around in the woods and along the creeks."

Whatever the reason, Poudlum and I didn't care. I could tell by his big grin that he was just as elated as I was about the adventure my uncle had made possible for us.

The old truck ground to a halt as its tires crunched on the gravel in front of Miss Lena's Store.

"Let's go in and talk to Lena for a spell," Uncle Curvin said as he fished around the floorboard searching for his walking stick. "I'll treat you little fellers to a cold drink."

I selected a peach Nehi and Poudlum got a strawberry. We were sitting up on the red drink box slowly sipping on them while we listened to Miss Lena and Uncle Curvin talk.

She was leaning on her counter between the cash register and a big round wooden case holding a hoop of cheese when she said, "Ain't you worried, Curvin, to be going up there in that courtroom and testifying against them bank robbers?"

My uncle replied to Miss Lena about the same way he had to Poudlum and me earlier, telling her, "I won't be no more scared than I was when they were pointing that big scattergun at me during the robbery."

Miss Lena didn't wear any lipstick or rouge, but she was still a pretty woman. Before she said anything else she took two big coconut cookies out of a large round glass jar, walked around from behind the counter and gave them to Poudlum and me to go with our drinks. She normally sold those cookies for two cents each.

On her way back to her accustomed place behind the counter she said to Uncle Curvin, "Well, ain't you scared that once they get out of prison they'll come back here looking for the people who testified against them and put them there?"

"Naw, I ain't scared of that," Uncle Curvin said. "Say, Lena, would you cut me a slice of that hoop cheese? Make it real thin cause you know I can't chew it."

Uncle Curvin had begun devouring his cheese when Lena said, "It seems like old Judge Garrison could put that trial off till after the holidays. It'll be Christmas before you know it. I know them folks on the jury won't appreciate being tied up right up till Christmas Day."

"He's too mule-headed to care about that, Lena. Having that trial is like a Christmas present to him."

"What's that solicitor's name?" Lena asked.

"That would be Danny Pierce, Old Man Alton and Mrs. Vera's boy."

"Is he any count?"

"I suppose he's as good as any other government worker, but in my opinion he wouldn't never make it on his own as a lawyer."

"Did you see the bank robbers during the arraignment?" Lena asked.

"Yeah, I seen them both up real close."

"Did they look scared?"

"Not those two. They just both sat there grinning like a mule eating briars."

"Why you think they were doing that?"

"Probably 'cause don't nobody know where the money is except them," Uncle Curvin answered.

Poudlum and I just about choked on our Nehis when he said that. They both glanced over our way, but I faked a cough, and we both sat up straight and just sat there swinging our legs off the drink box.

Uncle Curvin had finished his cheese and was ready to go. "Come on boys, make haste and I'll take y'all home."

"Wait a minute, Curvin," Miss Lena called out. "Do them bank robbers have themselves a lawyer?"

Uncle Curvin stopped in his crippled tracks, but didn't answer her right off.

"Well?" Miss Lena said.

Reluctantly, Uncle Curvin said, "Yeah, they got themselves a lawyer."

"Well, who is it?" She asked with a look in her eyes as if she already knew. "Is it who I'm thinking it is, Curvin?"

My uncle signed and said, "Yeah, it's him."

I hesitated to interrupt the conversation of two grown-ups, but I couldn't stand it anymore. "Who in the world are y'all talking about, Uncle Curvin?"

"I'm talking about that sorry, no-count, slick as a weasel, Old Man Alfred Jackson, that's who."

"He may be all that and more," Miss Lena said. "But you know and I know he don't never lose a court case."

I was confused. "Y'all mean that just 'cause Jesse and—uh, them bank robbers have this Mister Jackson as their lawyer, they might get away with robbing the bank?"

Miss Lena giggled, and said, "That's exactly what I'm thinking."

"Naw, not this time, Lena," Uncle Curvin said.

"Who dis Mister Jackson is?" Poudlum asked.

"Cut me another sliver of that cheese, would you, Lena?" my uncle said as he sank back down in the straight chair next to her counter where he proceeded to give us a detailed account of Jesse and Frank's legal counsel.

"I went to school with him many years ago," my uncle began. "He was always smart as a whip. When we finished school he went up north somewhere to some highbrow Yankee university, I believe it was in the state of Pennsylvania. Folks said he was a lawyer way up yonder for many years. Then about twenty years ago he come back down here, moved back into his family's old place, and opened hisself up a little law office."

Miss Lena chimed in and said, "And has been making fools out of county solicitors ever since by getting every client he's ever defended off scot-free."

"Was he ever de lawyer for any colored folks?" Poudlum inquired.

"Oh yeah," my uncle answered. "The one thing he seems to prefer to represent over anything else is a case when some darkie is accused of something. Why just a few months ago he got a colored feller off clean who was accused of stealing fertilizer from the feed and seed store. But this bank robber trial is pretty shut and closed. They did it, and me and some others saw 'em do it. I don't see no way how he can get 'em off."

Miss Lena shook her head and said, "Don't you be putting none of your money on that, Curvin."

During the ride home Uncle Curvin told Poudlum and me to wear our Sunday best because everybody dressed up when they went to court.

After supper that night my brother Fred and I lay in bed whispering our secrets to each other. We didn't have to worry about Ned because he was off chasing girls somewhere.

I whispered to him how Poudlum and I thought we

had solved Frank's riddle and figured the money was at the bottom of the Cypress Hole.

He told me he would go over there and dive down in the water and get it.

"No!" I whispered. "You can't go over there and do that. At least not until me and Poudlum can go with you and take along a piece of rope to tie around you. We going up to the courthouse tomorrow, so just wait, okay?"

"All right then, I'll wait."

"You promise?"

"Yeah, I promise," he said as he rolled over and gathered our quilt up around his chin.

I knew he was sleepy and it wasn't long before I heard him snoring softly. I also knew his promise was as good as gold, but before snuggling down into my sleeping position I took one last peek out the open window. There was my favorite star twinkling like a bright jewel on a dark velvet blanket of sky. I concentrated on it and made my wish, that my daddy would be home soon. He would know what to do.

Then I snuggled a little deeper and drifted into a safe and restful sleep like I hadn't in a good long time.

The morning sounds came drifting in like fog into a low meadow. Everyone was up except me and I could faintly hear the voices of my brothers and my mother coming from toward the kitchen. I couldn't make out a sentence, but an occasional distinguishable word alerted me that breakfast was about to be put on the table.

Afterwards, the ride to town wasn't too uncomfortable, bouncing around in my uncle's old truck. And the time had passed real fast, too. I supposed it was because of the anticipation of being able to attend the trial with my two best friends.

I was sitting in the middle and Poudlum had the window seat. I liked that arrangement because occasionally my uncle would let me shift the gear for him when he mashed the clutch down. The gear shift came straight up from the hump in the middle of the floor board. It was a straight metal rod with a round knob on the end of it. A knob that fit just right in your palm when you spread your fingers and thumb around it and shifted it into the invisible position while the clutch was pressed down.

The knob on the shift stick was cream-colored and had uncountable little hairline cracks running through it, with no particular pattern.

We were less than a mile from Grove Hill when the old truck began to choke going up a hill. Uncle Curvin mashed in the clutch and said, "All right, shift it up into second."

Using the knob, I pushed the gear stick straight up until I felt it hit neutral, and then a little further until I felt it drop into second gear. When the clutch was released the gear grabbed and the engine growled lower as it climbed on up the hill.

After we crested the hilltop he pressed the clutch in again and I shifted back into high gear and we cruised right on into town and parked between two painted lines on the asphalt next to the great and grand courthouse. It was bigger than I remembered it when back in the summer Poudlum and I had ridden up there to the cotton gin, and then on down into town when we had parked next to that statue of a Confederate soldier. That time we had been searching for candy and comic books. This time we were searching for justice for two bank robbers.

It was the biggest room I had ever seen, that courtroom. Uncle Curvin pointed everything out to us in a whispered tone. The raised bench where the judge sat, the little section of twelve seats where the jury would be enclosed, the table where the accused would sit with their lawyer, and the table where the county solicitor would sit.

He explained that the solicitor represented the state and would be presenting evidence to convince the jury that Jesse and Frank had indeed robbed the bank. Uncle Curvin said that he had been served with a subpoena, the official document informing him his presence was required in court as a witness for the state.

Then we all went back out in the hallway to sit on a bench and wait. The courthouse was already getting crowded. It was Tuesday, December 21, just four days before Christmas, and most people were off work for the rest of the week. I overheard one of the folks coming in with us say, "I can't believe that old fool judge scheduled this trial right here before Christmas."

I was startled when Uncle Curvin stood up and told us, "You boys just go in and watch things. I got to go now."

I was alarmed to hear that. "Where you going? You gonna leave us here by ourselves?"

"Y'all will be all right. I got to go sit in the witness room till they call me, but we'll all be able to get us some dinner when the judge breaks at noon. I might just buy y'all a hamburger."

After he disappeared down the hall Poudlum and I pulled

the massive door open and slipped into the courtroom un-
noticed, only to find ourselves in an awkward position. All
the white folks were sitting up front and the colored folks
were all on the two back rows.

I wanted us to sit together, but for a moment just didn't
know how to handle the situation. Finally I nudged Poudlum
and nodded toward some empty space on the very back row.
I figured nobody would notice a white boy and a colored
boy sitting together way back there.

We sat there for a while and watched the courtroom fill
up with people and pretty soon it was filled to capacity and
a lot of people had to stand and were leaning against the
wall when a man Uncle Curvin had pointed out earlier as
the bailiff barked out, "All rise!"

I was in awe of the whole situation when I felt Poudlum
tugging on my jacket sleeve whispering, "Reckon we better
stand up, everybody else is."

The judge, who had entered the courtroom from a door
back behind the raised place he sat, had on a big, flowing black robe. He made his way up to his seat, sat down,
and looked around the courtroom for what seemed like
an unnecessarily long time before he told everyone to be
seated.

"Old goat," I heard someone toward the front mutter
during the rustling noise as everyone sat down.

The courtroom got real quiet when another door over on
the left side of the courtroom opened and an armed deputy
led the two prisoners through it. Poudlum and I both caught
our breath when we saw Jesse and Frank shuffling into the
courtroom while the chains on their feet rattled and scraped

on the floor. They had handcuffs on their wrists, too.

"Now dey knows what it's like to be trussed up like a hog," Poudlum leaned over and whispered. "Dey don't look no worse for de wear though."

I had to admit he was correct. Jesse and Frank looked fat and sassy; in fact, they were leaning over and whispering to each other, grinning and smirking while they sat alone at the defense table.

The jury began filing in from the other side of the courtroom and all took their seats in the designated area for jurors.

Judge Garrison glanced all about the courtroom like my uncle would look out over his cotton patch to see if everything was in order and everyone was ready to start picking.

His eyes froze when he got to the defense table. I knew he was mad when he shouted, "Does anyone know where the counsel for the defense—"

He was interrupted when the double doors leading into the courtroom burst open, and a man dressed like a preacher with flowing white hair and a trimmed white beard came walking into the courtroom like he was the cock of the roost.

"Uh-oh," I heard someone say. "Here comes Mr. Alfred Jackson!"

Chapter Fourteen

THE BREAKOUT

M r. Jackson didn't waste any time living up to his reputation. He started a big ruckus right off the bat. After he dropped his old weathered briefcase on the defense table, he observed the two prisoners in their striped prison garb for a few moments while the courtroom grew so quiet you could have heard a church mouse scurrying across the floor.

The crowd in the courtroom, including the judge and jury, collectively held their breath while they awaited his first move.

It didn't take him long. He turned away from his clients and faced Judge Garrison as he put his hands on his hips and let out a long audible sigh while he shook his head back and forth. "Your honor," he said. "May it please the court, to inform me why my clients are shackled in chains and wearing jailhouse attire?"

Without allowing the startled judge to answer, he continued, "This is clearly a ploy by the solicitor to present them in this incriminating manner before the jury. These men are innocent until such time as they are proven guilty beyond a reasonable doubt, yet they are presented here as if they are already convicted criminals. As citizens of this great country they deserve their day in court just as much as you or I would. Now I demand they be unshackled and allowed to change into proper courtroom attire!"

If possible, the courtroom grew even quieter as everyone turned their eyes toward Judge Garrison, awaiting his reaction.

It was like the judge was in a trance for a few moments before he finally began sputtering and stuttering and blurted out, "Will-will-will counsel please approach the bench!"

Mr. Pierce, the solicitor, and Mr. Jackson both immediately went up and leaned their heads real close while the judge leaned over and joined them in a private conversation.

A buzz began rippling through the courtroom while they whispered. But then the judge's head jerked up and he began to pound on the bench with his gavel. Bang! Bang! Bang! The sharp sound of it reverberated across the courtroom and silence set in once again while his eyes swept across the crowd, looking for a dissenter.

He didn't find one and he and the lawyers went back to their whispering. Finally he rapped his gavel again, gently this time, just before he said. "We'll be taking a ten-minute recess. Bailiff! Remove the prisoners from the courtroom."

Poudlum and I sat real still and observed while everyone began talking in hushed tones while all the officers of the court, and the jury, left the courtroom. I overheard someone say, "How can we take a recess when we ain't even started yet?"

It wasn't long before the bailiff walked back into the courtroom and shouted again, "All rise!"

Everyone settled back down in their seats after the judge came back and allowed it. The jury filed back in after that, and then, lo and behold, the side door opened and Mr. Jackson came through it followed by Jesse and Frank who were free of any chains and were both dressed in suits and ties, just like the lawyers.

Once again a murmur rippled through the crowd and someone across from us said, "Round one goes to Mr. Jackson!"

Judge Garrison began pounding his gavel again and threatened to clear the courtroom. That got everybody quiet and the trial finally got underway.

Mr. Pierce spent the entire morning presenting his first two witnesses, the bank manager and the teller who had been waiting on Uncle Curvin when the robbery occurred. They both pointed out Jesse and Frank as the robbers on several occasions while Mr. Jackson just sat at the defense table scribbling on a tablet of paper the entire time and declined to cross-examine either witness.

Once again, I heard someone up toward the front say real low, "He's got something up his sleeve, I'll guarantee it."

Poudlum and I weren't quite sure what to do when the judge declared a lunch break, but then Uncle Curvin appeared and told us to come on with him because he was going to buy us that hamburger he had promised.

Once outside, we walked up to the Freezette and watched

while he stood in line and came away with a white paper bag containing our food. They didn't have any Nehis so he got us all three Coca-Colas and we walked back down to my uncle's truck where he let the tailgate down and we sat on it to take our meal.

It was a good burger, juicy, with lots of ketchup, mustard, and mayonnaise. "Is yours good, Poudlum?" I asked between bites.

"Shore is," he replied. "'Bout de second-best thing I ever had to eat."

"What was the first best thing?" Uncle Curvin inquired as he sipped on a cup of chili.

"Catfish," Poudlum replied without hesitation. "Fried catfish outta de Cypress Hole on de Satilfa," he added as juice from the burger dribbled down his chin.

As we were finishing up I asked my uncle, "How come you hadn't had to testify yet?"

"They just didn't get around to me yet. I expect I'll be the next one when we start back."

"Is you scared, Mister Curvin?" Poudlum asked.

"Naw, I ain't scared at all, son. I'm ready to do my duty. Now y'all wipe your mouths. I reckon it's time to be getting back in there."

I pulled my jacket tighter as we walked up the courthouse steps because I could feel a chill. It seemed like the temperature was getting a lot colder.

Poudlum and I settled into our original seats while the crowd filed back in toward the front of us. We were in our seats watching the courtroom come to order once again when I got a feeling something was about to happen.

Poudlum felt it, too. I could tell by the roundness of his eyes. Involuntarily we both grabbed hold of the back of the bench in front of us in anticipation of we didn't know what. But somehow we both knew that something was about to bust loose in the courtroom.

I don't know why, but Poudlum and I got a mutual feeling when bad, strange, or unusual things were about to happen, and we had learned to prepare for them. This time we both hunkered down in our seats with nothing but our eyes and the tops of our heads above the edge of the back of the bench in front of us.

Mr. Pierce stood up and said, "Your honor, at this time the prosecution would like to call Mr. Curvin—"

"Hold it! Just hold it right there, Mr. Pierce," the judge interrupted.

Looking toward the defense table, he said to Mr. Jackson, "Counselor, would you mind informing the court where your clients are?"

"I'm sure I don't know, your honor. My job is to defend them, not nursemaid them."

That made the judge mad. "You keep a respectful tongue in your head, Mr. Jackson, or I'll have you up on contempt!" the judge responded, so angry his voice betrayed a slight tremble. "Bailiff!" he yelled.

There was only one bailiff in the courtroom, leaning against the wall next to the jury box. The one who had escorted the prisoners in and out of the courtroom was nowhere to be seen. The one who was present snapped out of his slumped position and quickly stepped in front of the bench facing the judge.

"Yes, sir, Your Honor," he sputtered.

The judge gave him stern directions to proceed to the prisoners' holding area and escort the prisoners into the courtroom along with the missing bailiff.

When the bailiff left the courtroom, once again, it got real quiet with everyone halfway holding their breath.

The solicitor was sitting in his seat tapping his pencil on the table in frustration while he stared at the door where the prisoners should be coming through. The folks in the jury box were shuffling around in their seats, some of them leaning over and whispering to each other.

After a few moments the crowd in the courtroom began to get restless again and a low murmur of uncertainty and curiosity began to sweep through them, that is, until the judge rapped his gavel again and swept his stern gaze across the breadth of the courtroom.

Everyone's attention became riveted to the side door when the bailiff who had just left the courtroom on the judge's errand timidly eased the side door open and came back into the courtroom in a manner that indicated he didn't really want to, with a pained expression on his face.

After a brief moment, Judge Garrison yelled, "Well?"

"They—they gone, Your Honor!" the bailiff stuttered.

It looked like the judge's head was going to explode his face got so red. "Just who are you referring to as 'gone,' bailiff?" he shouted.

"The—the prisoners, Your Honor," he replied in a voice just above a whisper.

The judge leaned toward him and demanded, "Speak up, man!"

"I said the two prisoners, Your Honor, they both gone!"

Mr. Pierce, the solicitor, leapt to his feet and shouted at the bailiff, "Where's the other bailiff and the deputy?"

"They both back there in the holding area, sir," he meekly replied.

Mr. Jackson just sat there at the defense table, still scribbling on a legal pad.

Now the judge was on his feet. "Well, what are they doing in the holding cell, bailiff?" he shouted out.

"They both just laying there on the floor all tied up, you honor."

"Tied up?"

"Yes, sir."

"Tied up with what? They need to be in this courtroom!"

"They tied up with the neckties the prisoners were wearing, your honor."

Bedlam brook loose in the courtroom. The judge was banging his gavel, the solicitor was shaking his fist and yelling at Mr. Jackson, "This is all your fault, sir!"

The crowd was surging through the double doors leading from the courtroom while the judge kept beating his gavel and shouting, "Order, order in this court!"

Poudlum nudged me and asked, "What you think we ought to do?"

"Let's go out to the truck and wait on Uncle Curvin," I told him.

When we got outside the first thing we saw was the sheriff's car come tearing around from behind the courthouse and take off down toward Coffeeville.

First a bank robbery, then a trial, and now a jailbreak. All right before Christmas. It was almost too much for the folks outside the courthouse to stand.

We hung around town with Uncle Curvin until well after sundown. A lot of people were milling around to see if they caught Frank and Jesse and brought them back to jail.

It began to get cold, I mean real cold. After all, it was only a few days before Christmas, and it was way past time for some cold weather to set in. Uncle Curvin pulled his old dungaree jacket out from behind the seat of his truck and slipped it on while he shivered and talked to folks still hanging around the parking lot of the courthouse.

Poudlum and I had only worn our light jackets so we got inside the cab of the truck and rolled up the windows. It wasn't real warm, but it was better than being outside. "When you think Mister Curvin gon head on toward home?" Poudlum asked.

"I believe it won't be long," I told him. "Lots of folks done gone home and give up on Jesse and Frank being brought back in."

"Dat was real sneaky de way dey got away," Poudlum said.

"Yeah it was. You know where they heading, don't you?"

"Uh-huh, dey probably heading to de Cypress Hole to pull dat money out of de water."

"Naw, it'll be too cold and dark for them to get it tonight."

"Yeah, you is probably right, but what about tomorrow.

Dey will probably get dat money and it'll be gone forever. We should've tried to get it soon as you found dat arrow carved in dey black gum tree. Should've got it while de gettin' was good."

About that time the door of the truck opened and Uncle Curvin hobbled inside and closed the door. "You boys about ready to get on home? I don't think nothing else is going to happen around here tonight."

"Yes, sir, we 'bout freezing," Poudlum said.

"Yep, it do seem like we a fixing to have us a cold snap," Uncle Curvin said while he was cranking up the truck. "It'll get warm in here once we get the motor running for a while."

He put the gear in reverse and backed us out of our parking space. That's when I noticed the first few drops of rain spattering on the windshield. The glass had some cracks in it and had faded around the edges with a milky-white tone, but I could definitely see fine rain flowing over the cracks and down onto the hood.

We were barely out of town when the first welcome warm air came blowing up from the floorboard to warm our cold feet and hands. Then the fine rain began to make a clicking and popping sound on the metal hood and the glass windshield.

My uncle turned on the windshield wipers and said, "I do believe we got some sleet coming down on us, boys. Doggone, I wish we had left earlier."

It got heavier as we went along. Uncle Curvin kept pulling his handkerchief out of his pocket to wipe the fog off the inside of the windshield, and a steady peppering sound permeated the cozy cab of the truck as the sleet got thicker and beat down on us with a sound like hard rain on dry leaves.

Pretty soon I was having a difficult time seeing the road through the windshield because the sleet was beginning to come down harder and thicker.

"I ain't seen nothing like this in quite a spell," my uncle said as he mopped the fog off the windshield in front of him.

"I can't see nothing. Where is we Mister Curvin?" Poudlum asked.

"I can't see too much myself, but I can tell we fixing to turn off the paved road onto Center Point Road, and it ain't but seven or eight more miles to home."

After we had crept along for about a mile Uncle Curvin rolled his window down. The damp, frigid air came rushing in while he stuck his head out the window and maneuvered the truck off on the side of the road. "I can't see good enough to drive anymore, boys. Let's just sit here for awhile and see if it'll slack up."

He rolled his window up, cut off the engine and the lights, and it immediately got colder in the truck. "I'll crank the motor up every once in a while and warm us up," he promised while Poudlum and I scrunched up close to each other. "Reach back there behind the seat and there's an old army blanket. Pull it out and y'all can wrap up in it. It'll keep you little fellers warm."

The old blanket was rough and stiff, but it was a welcome buffer against the increasing cold after Poudlum and I spread it over us and tucked in the edges all around us.

"Y'all warm now?" Uncle Curvin asked.

"A little bit," I told him. "But it's still real cold."

"I got to see what time it is," Uncle Curvin said as he struck a wooden match so he could see his pocket watch.

When the flare of the match lit up the cab of the truck, Poudlum said, "I can see yo' breath."

"Huh?"

"Yo' breath, I can see it when you breathes out. It's all frosty and white. You knows it's cold when you can see yo' breath."

We sat there and shivered in silence for a while. Then Poudlum said, "I think my nose gon fall off it's so cold."

"All right," Uncle Curvin said. "I'll crank up the engine and warm us up."

Not long afterwards it got toasty warm in the truck. While the engine was running I noticed the little circle on the dashboard that was the gas gauge. The needle was just barely above the empty mark. After my uncle cut the engine off I asked him, "How much gas you think we got left?"

I could hear the concern in his voice when he replied, "Not nearly enough as we probably gonna need to get through this cold night."

CHAPTER FIFTEEN

STRANDED

If Uncle Curvin had had any teeth they would have been chattering like mine and Poudlum's. The sleet kept pouring down and ice was beginning to accumulate around the windshield wipers.

"I'm going to start the motor one more time and warm us up a little, boys," my uncle said. "But they ain't enough gas to do it many more times."

"You got any more of dem matches, Mister Curvin?" Poudlum asked.

"Uh-huh, I got plenty of matches, but they won't keep us warm."

"Dey would if we built us a fire," Poudlum told him.

"We can't build no fire, son, what with ice coming down like it is."

"I knows a dry place nearby where we could get one going."

Poudlum had my attention now. "What you talking about, Poudlum?"

"If we could use what gas we got left to make it to the Satilfa, we could get up under de bridge and build us a fire."

Uncle Curvin straightened up in the seat and said, "Why that's about the most sensible thing I heard all day, including everything they said in the courtroom.

"It's gonna be a cold ride," he said as he started the engine of the truck and rolled down his window. "I'll have to hang out the window to see. Y'all just wrap up real tight in that blanket and we'll see if we can make it to the bridge."

There was a long downhill grade for about half of a mile before the road got to the Satilfa Creek Bridge. About halfway down it the old truck ran out of gas, sputtered and went dead. Uncle Curvin shifted the gear into neutral and said, "I think we can coast on down to the bridge. Y'all just hang on."

The road leveled out and the truck coasted to a halt about a hundred yards from the bridge. Uncle Curvin rolled up his window and said, "We gonna have to walk the rest of the way. Y'all bring the blanket along with you."

The sleet pelted us pretty good on the walk down to the bridge. When we got to it Uncle Curvin said, "I'll hold the light to show us the way, you boys just follow me, and be careful 'cause it's starting to get a little slick."

"Don't you worry about a thing," I told him as Poudlum and I grabbed hold of each other while we climbed down the bank as Uncle Curvin lit the way. It was treacherous, but we made it by grabbing hold of small pine trees with our free hands.

It was cold and eerie when we got under the bridge. Everything was still and the only sounds were the swish of the creek as it went by and the peppering sound of the sleet on the bridge above us.

"If we get up in the secret place and build us a fire in it we can stay warm all night," I whispered to Poudlum.

"Shore can," he whispered back. "But yo' brother ain't gon be happy about us showing it to Mister Curvin."

"Naw, I don't think he'll care. He'll understand it was something we had to do."

"What y'all a-whispering about?" Uncle Curvin demanded.

"We'll show you," I told him as I took his flashlight and pointed it up toward the secret place my brother had discovered. We struggled a bit, but we finally tumbled into the secret place.

Uncle Curvin took his flashlight back and cast the beam about inside it. "Good Lord!" he declared. "This is some kind of nice hidey hole. Why we can build us just a little fire in here and be as warm as if we was in your momma's kitchen.

A few minutes later we had us a nice fire going with a large stack of fuel, enough to last us through the frozen night. The walls of the secret place trapped the heat and with the blanket we had brought from the truck the numbness began to disappear from my fingers and toes. It got warmer still, and I knew we were going to be all right.

Uncle Curvin took his jacket off, rolled it up and used it as a pillow as he stretched out. "I believe we gonna be all right boys, thanks to this here hidey hole of y'all's. This storm will break and come tomorrow morning we'll walk on out of here toward home."

The warmth of the fire, the sound of the sleet peppering down on the bridge above us, and the cozy feeling of the secret place combined to put a real drowsy feeling on me. I glanced over toward Poudlum and saw his eyelids were getting heavy, too.

I added a few more pieces of fuel to the fire, and pretty soon I got so toasty warm in the hidey hole that Poudlum and I kicked off the blanket we had been sharing.

We made us a pillow out of it and stretched out like Uncle Curvin next to the warm embers and pretty soon I felt myself drifting off. It had been a long day, and even though I was in a strange place and sleeping on the hard ground instead of in my warm, comfortable bed, I still felt secure being there with Poudlum and Uncle Curvin, so sleep came easily and soon I fell into a deep sleep.

Just before dawn Poudlum shook me gently awake. "What's the matter?" I asked, rubbing my eyes as I sat up.

"Shhh," Poudlum whispered. "Be real quiet."

"What is it?" I whispered back.

"Dey is somebody walking up on de bridge," he said in a whisper.

"It ain't even daylight yet. Who could it be?" I whispered.

"Who you think?" Poudlum answered in a low growl.

The sleet had turned to a soft drizzle, but through the soft sound of it I heard heavy footsteps on the wooden planks up above, and knew Poudlum was correct. It sounded like maybe two people.

"You think they can see our fire?"

"Naw, it ain't nothing but hot coals covered with white

ashes. We better wake up Mister Curvin, but be real quiet about it."

The sound of steps on the bridge stopped, but then the rustle and scraping sound of them coming down the bank toward the creek started.

"Don't wake him up yet," I told Poudlum. "Let's make sure who it is first."

"You know it's gonna be Jesse and Frank," Poudlum responded.

"Well, let's just make sure."

We both eased up and peeked over the wall of the secret place and in the pre-dawn dimness we both recognized the faint outlines of Jesse and Frank as they reached the creek bank just below the bridge and across the creek from us. We continued to observe until they disappeared into the woods heading up the creek toward the Cypress Hole.

"Dey going to get de money!" Poudlum hissed. "We ought to got it ourselves when we had de chance!"

I knew Poudlum was probably right, but I also knew we had to get up on the road and get gone because they had surely seen Uncle Curvin's truck and suspected we were somewhere close by.

I figured they were probably out of hearing distance by now, especially with the sound of the drizzle, so I moved over close to Uncle Curvin and slowly shook his shoulder until he roused up.

He snorted and wheezed just before I leaned down and whispered into his ear and said, "Uncle Curvin, you need to wake up. Them bank robbers are just up the creek from us!"

"Are you dreaming, boy, or am I?" he said from a prone position.

"Neither one, we got to get up and get out of here while we can!"

"You seen 'em?"

"Yes, sir. Poudlum heard them up on the bridge and woke me up. Then we watched them climb down the bank and head up the creek toward the Cypress Hole."

Uncle Curvin sat up slowly and said, "I can't move too fast. Besides being cripple, I'm cold and stiff from sleeping on this hard ground. Maybe you boys ought to light out and leave me here."

"No, sir, Mister Curvin," Poudlum piped up. "We can't leave you here by yo'self."

He sat up and scooted over a little closer to the bed of ashes, which still had some hot coals radiating heat. "Listen, boys, by the time y'all pulled me out of this warm hidey hole and helped me up to the bank it would probably be broad daylight. I'll be fine here. The thing to do is for y'all to scamper on out of here real quiet-like and go get us some help. Y'all can leave that blanket with me, though."

It didn't take Poudlum and me but a few moments to realize he was right.

"All right," I told him. "You just stay low in here. Me and Poudlum will get up on the road and run all the way to Uncle Curtis's house and wake him up. He'll know what to do."

"Uh, before you go, boys, what do y'all think the bank robbers are doing here on the creek. I would have thought they would have been clean out of the county by now."

Poudlum looked at me and said, "Might as well tell him."

I knew Poudlum was right. It was too late to be keeping secrets now. "They come back to get the money," I told him.

"Huh?"

"Yes, sir, we think they got the money sunk up there in the Cypress Hole."

"Well now why in the world would y'all think something like that?"

"Tell him real quick," Poudlum said. "Then we gots to get on outta here."

After I quickly told my uncle the whole story culminating when we had found the arrow carved into the black gum tree, he said, "Lord, have mercy! You boys should have done told me about all that. In fact, y'all should have been testifying in court!"

"We wuz scared, Mister Curvin. Plus, we wuz after dat reward money," Poudlum told him.

"I can understand that, boys, and it's all right. But now y'all need to get up on the road and run."

Poudlum and I slithered out of the secret place like two snakes. We lowered ourselves to the ground and crept out from under the bridge. But when we took our first step up the bank we were shocked when we slid right back down. The bank was a sheet of ice from the sleet.

"Uh oh, what we gon do now?" Poudlum whispered.

Thinking fast, I told him, "Feel around and find a good stick. We'll break them so they got sharp ends and stab them in the ground and pull ourselves up.

I heard a sharp crack when Poudlum broke his stick, and mine followed. "You think dey heard dat?" he asked.

"Probably did, let's start climbing."

The sticks worked well enough and soon I felt my hands on the crusty sheet of ice on the ditch next to the road. I pulled myself up and Poudlum was right behind me.

We stood there on the side of Center Point Road in the predawn light for a few moments, breathing hard.

"You hear anything?" I whispered with a frosty breath.

We listened real hard for a few moments before Poudlum said, "Naw, does you?"

"No, me neither," I responded. "Let's start running!"

It was so cold it hurt to breathe, but we ran hard until we got to the Mill Creek Bridge, where we stopped to catch our breath. "You okay?" I asked Poudlum.

"Uh-huh, I'm rested. Let's see how far we can run fo' we has to stop again."

It was uphill all the way from the Mill Creek Bridge to Uncle Curtis's house and Poudlum and I were both blowing like a mule pulling a ground slide loaded with watermelons by the time we got there. But we weren't cold anymore; in fact, we were both damp with perspiration.

We turned off the road down toward Uncle Curtis's house and I could see a light inside when we got to the front porch.

There was a smell of bacon frying and it made my mouth water. I knew Poudlum was experiencing the same feeling when I glanced toward him and saw his eyes roll while he licked his lips.

We told the story of our all-night vigil, including the bank robber's visit, to Uncle Curtis while he served us up some thick sliced bacon along with some fried eggs with syrup and biscuits.

Afterwards, he told my cousin Robert to go crank up the truck and get it warm. Shortly after that, while Poudlum and I soaked up the warmth of the inside of the cab, we drove down to Miss Lena's Store.

To our surprise, there was a small crowd of people gathered there. It seemed that Poudlum's momma and daddy, my two brothers and my own momma, plus a few other folks had all gathered there for the purpose of finding us and Uncle Curvin.

After everybody fussed over us for a while, Uncle Curtis and some others headed back up Center Point Road to go rescue Uncle Curvin, and some others headed off toward Coffeeville to find a telephone to call the sheriff and tell him the escaped bank robbers had been sighted.

Things got kind of fuzzy after that. I remember being on a pallet on the floor in front of our warm fireplace covered with a quilt. I felt my momma's cool, soft hand on my burning forehead and heard her voice sounding like it was coming from somewhere way off when she said, "This child's burning up with fever."

I drifted in and out of consciousness, sometimes sleeping lightly, sometimes deeply, but I woke up clearheaded on Thursday morning, so hungry I felt like my belly was scraping my backbone.

"We thought you had pneumonia for a while," my momma said. "But you just got chilled real bad after you sweated through your clothes with all that running in the freezing cold."

"Has anybody heard from Poudlum?" I asked while I sopped up syrup with a hot biscuit.

"He's been sick, too," my momma told me. "At least that's what your brother Fred heard from over at Miss Lena's Store."

"Where are they?" I asked her. "Ned and Fred?"

"They both out cutting firewood to get us through this cold spell. Now you finish up your meal and get back under them covers for a while."

The fire had died down to a bed of hot coals when I crawled back into my pallet. With my belly full, I propped up on a pillow, pulled the quilt up over me and watched as Momma piled fresh logs on the fire.

Pretty soon little blue and yellow flames began to spring up from the bed of coals and lick up between the cracks of the logs like flaming cat tongues. It wasn't long before the flames leapt higher and the fire turned into a roaring and popping solid blaze, radiating heat that lulled me back to sleep.

The rumble and thump of wood being stacked on the floor next to the fireplace woke me up.

I looked up, sleepy-eyed, and saw my brother Ned grinning down toward me. "You gonna sleep all day?" he asked as he reached down and rumpled my hair. "Wake up, Fred's got something you'll be wanting to see."

I heard a rattling and crinkling of paper as Fred sat down next to me. "Move over," he said. "Quit hogging the fire and I'll show you this story in the *Clarke County Democrat*."

What he had was the weekly county newspaper. It came out every Thursday. "Look here on the front page," he said.

The cobwebs disappeared from my mind and my eyes bugged out when I saw the headline.

CHAPTER SIXTEEN

THE ROPE

The headline read: "Bank Robbers Recaptured, Money Still Missing."

"They caught 'em!" I gasped.

"Yep," Fred confirmed. "They caught 'em 'bout froze to death right there at the Cypress Hole. I heard they was wet and so cold they were almost glad to be caught again."

"But—but what about the money? It says the money's still missing. They didn't have it?"

Fred didn't answer, but my brother Ned chimed in. "Nobody found no money. The bank robbers said they had sunk it in the Cypress Hole and they were there trying to pull it out of the water. They claimed to have tied a rope to the base of a black gum tree, which did have a mark carved into it, and sunk the money in a waterproof rubber bag, but they said there wasn't no signs of the rope when they got there."

"What you 'spect happened to it?" I asked.

"Everybody thinks the rope probably came loose and the bag of money washed on down the Satilfa," Ned said.

My fever was gone and I was thinking clearly now. I knew that Poudlum and I should have gone after that money when we first figured out where it was. We just hadn't thought to dig down into the leaves and look for a rope. We wouldn't have had to go into that cold, deep water after all. We could have just found the rope and pulled that money up and be rich now. We had figured everything out except that last little simple detail.

"Do y'all think that really happened?" I asked. "I mean that the rope came loose and the money floated on down the creek?"

"Half the folks in the county seem to think so," Ned told me. "They's folks trampling all up and down the creek in the freezing cold looking for it all the way down to where it runs into the Tombigbee."

I felt kind of like when you spill your last glass of milk, or lose your best friend. "Do y'all think anybody will find it?" I asked.

Fred was throwing some good hickory logs on the fire when he said, "Nope, I don't think anybody is going to find anything."

It wasn't long after that before our momma ran us all to bed. She said she thought I was well enough to get off my sick pallet and get in my regular bed.

It was cold in our room, and Fred and I drew up two quilts and tucked them up under our chins, and it wasn't long before we got good and warm, But I wasn't sleepy and something my brother had said was still bothering me. "You still awake?" I whispered to Fred.

"Uh-huh," he answered softly.

Brother Ned, across the room in his bed, was snoring softly.

Before I could say anything else Fred sneezed and then coughed with a slight rattle in his throat.

"You ain't getting sick, are you?"

"I might be getting a little bit of a cold, but I'll be all right."

A cold, soft rain had begun outside. I liked it when it rained at night. The sound of distant thunder and the sound of the rain pinging on the tin roof always gave me a feeling of being snug and secure in my warm, dry bed. "What did you mean when you said ain't nobody gonna find anything looking down the creek?"

"I meant just what I said."

"But how you know they ain't gonna find the money floating down the creek or washed up on a sand bar somewhere?"

"'Cause I just do, now go to sleep," he said with a tone of finality in his voice that told me he wasn't going to talk anymore tonight.

I felt the bed move as he rolled over and settled into a final sleeping position, and I knew I wasn't going to get any more information out of him tonight.

Pretty soon he was snoring, too. Me, I was warm and cozy, but sleep was far from my mind. I supposed it was because I had been dozing on and off all day on my pallet in front of the fireplace.

It was one of those times when you think you can't go to sleep and the next thing you know it's the next morning. But when I awoke the same thought still lingered in my mind—that we had come so close and still let the money get away.

I had just noticed our room was empty except for me when my momma came in and asked me how I felt.

"I feel good," I told her. "Just hungry."

"Nothing unusual about that," she said. "Did you forget what day it is?"

"Ma'am?"

"Today's your birthday, son!"

I had plumb forgot. I was twelve years old today and Poudlum had turned twelve yesterday.

"I've got you a hot breakfast ready. When you finish eating I want you to go out to the henhouse and gather the eggs so I can make you a cake."

The thoughts of breakfast and cake was enough to get me out of bed.

While my momma was serving me fried eggs I asked her where my brothers were.

"They've gone with Curvin to cut firewood for the hog killing tomorrow. Looks like this freezing weather is going to be with us for a spell, so tomorrow will be a good time for it."

We didn't raise any hogs, but we always got a share of the meat because we all worked hard at it, especially my momma. She and Poudlum's momma cleaned the chitterlings and stuffed them with ground sausage and made the best link sausage around; they also made the best souse meat in the county. Everybody would be wanting a piece.

It turned out to be a grand birthday. Uncle Curvin came and ate supper with us. We all ate the cake Momma made for me. She stuck straws down into the layers while she applied the hot chocolate icing and it trickled all down into it so that when you sliced it you could see the dark streaks just waiting for you to bite into.

Fred gave me a new slingshot he had made, Ned gave me an arrowhead he had found and Uncle Curvin gave me a fifty-cent piece. After supper, topped off with chocolate cake, we all went off to bed early in anticipation of the excitement and camaraderie of the next morning.

Uncle Curtis always hosted the hog killings because he had a large level area in his backyard where several large, black wash pots could be set up with fires underneath them to boil the water used to scald the hogs.

The fires were already leaping high around the pots when we arrived. Several hogs had been butchered and were hanging upside down from a wooden beam between two oak trees. Besides harvesting meat to get through the winter, a hog killing was also a social event, but only relatives, neighbors, and good friends were invited to share in the work and the bounty.

I was glad when I spotted Poudlum warming himself next to one of the pots, but we didn't have an opportunity to talk right away because the water in the pots had begun to boil and it was our job to use big dippers to transfer the hot water from the pots and pour it on the hogs. We had to concentrate while performing this task because the slightest mistake and you could scald yourself instead of the pig.

Some other folks' job was to scrape the hair off the hogs after we poured the boiling water on them. The bitter cold didn't bother us since the heat from the fire and the hot steam from the boiling water warmed us.

My arms were aching after countless trips between the pots and the pigs, but soon those pigs were as clean, pink, and smooth as a baby's bottom.

The next step was to take the hogs down and place them on a large table where the men cut them up into hams, shoulders, pork chops, bacon, ribs, and sausage meat.

The hams, bacon, and link sausage were toted off and hung from the rafters of Uncle Curtis's smoke house where the smoke from small hickory fires would curl up and around to cure the meat.

About midmorning everyone gathered around one small pot and enjoyed a steamy bowl of stew made from the liver and lights.

Everyone would have fresh pork chops for breakfast, dinner, and supper the next day, and would share the cured ham, bacon, and sausage through the rest of the winter.

Things were kind of winding down by early afternoon. The only thing left going on was some ladies making souse meat and pickling the pig's feet in big jars.

That's when Poudlum and I finally got an opportunity to talk. We met at the one last pot with a fire going around it where the fat was being rendered down into lard for cooking. "You see the newspaper?" Poudlum asked.

"Yeah, I seen it," I answered dejectedly.

"Guess we should a got while de getting wuz good."

"Uh-huh, we sure should have. After all the trouble we went to and we didn't even think to scratch around the bottom of that tree and find the rope. All we would have had to do was just haul it up."

"I guess we ain't as smart as we thought, is we?"

"I guess not."

"I went to Coffeeville to de store wid my daddy yesterday and heard a lot of talk," Poudlum said.

"What did you hear?"

"Heard some folks saying the law had a crew of men dragging the Cypress Hole and working dey way on down de creek."

"Did they say how far they got?"

"Uh-huh, all de way down to de river, and dey ain't seen nary a dollar."

"Did you hear anything else?"

"Folks saying all kind of stuff, like de bank robbers probably hid dat money somewhere else and made up dat story about sinking it in de Cypress Hole just to throw folks off."

"I don't think I believe that, do you, Poudlum?"

"Uh-uh, 'cause it don't seem like dey would've gone to de trouble of carving dat arrow in de tree to mark de spot if dey hadn't left de money in de creek."

"Me neither. They could have just made up that story without carving that arrow. They weren't familiar with the creek and they wanted to mark that spot. We just happened to be fishing across the creek from where they decided to hide the money."

That's when Fred walked up. "What y'all doing?" he asked.

"Just trying to keep warm," I told him.

"Hey, Poudlum, I heard you just about froze to death the other night along with Ted and Uncle Curvin."

"Dat's right, it was mighty cold," Poudlum said. Then he glanced around to make sure no one was within hearing distance before he continued. "We probably would've froze to death if we hadn't of knowed about yo' secret place under de bridge."

Fred frowned a little frown and said, "Yeah, that may be true, but now Uncle Curvin knows about it. We might as well put a piece in the *Democrat* telling where it is."

"Naw!" I said. "Uncle Curvin won't say nothing. We told him it was a secret."

"I sure hope you're right about that. But listen, what I wanted to talk to y'all about was getting up another fishing trip for maybe this Sunday after church. We're going to be tired of eating this pig by then."

"It's too cold to go fishing!" I told him.

"It'll be good and warm by Sunday," Fred retorted.

"How you know dat?" Poudlum asked.

"I read it in *The Old Farmer's Almanac*. It predicted an extreme warming trend just before Christmas, and it's never wrong."

"How you think dey can figure out de weather like dat?" Poudlum asked.

"I'm not completely sure," Fred answered. "But what I think is they keep charts and graphs of what the weather had been like for years and years. And I think they can see cycles that happen and make predictions based on those cycles. Everything in nature happens in cycles, including the weather."

Poudlum looked at me and said, "How come yo' brother so smart and you and I is so dumb?"

"He ain't so smart, and we ain't dumb," I answered defensively.

"Y'all both real smart," Fred said in a conciliatory tone. "But y'all do need to listen to me on this occasion. Now what do you say? If I'm right and the weather warms up, do y'all want to go?"

I glanced toward Poudlum, he nodded and said, "If it really do get warm, I'm always ready to go fishing."

"All right," I told my brother. 'We'll go Sunday after church and stay all night on the Cypress Hole, if it really does get warm."

"It will," Fred said.

What he said next, just before he walked away, made Poudlum and me wonder just what my brother was up to. "Besides going fishing, I'll have a little surprise for y'all, kind of like a late birthday present for both of you."

He coughed like he had a cold and walked away from us and began helping over at the table where they were packing pork chops on ice.

"What you 'spect yo' brother be up to?" Poudlum asked.

"I ain't sure, but I think we ought to go along with him and see, especially if it's warm on Sunday."

"What you get for yo' birthday?" Poudlum asked.

After I told him I asked, "What about you?"

"I got me a dog!" he proudly announced.

"A dog? What kind?"

"He gray wid blue specks all over him. Got big old long ears. I can lap 'em over his head and cover his eyes, or even his nose. Plan to make a squirrel dog outta him, and wuz hoping you would let him hunt wid yo' dog, Bill."

"I would be proud for your puppy to hunt with Old Bill. After Christmas we'll get my brother Ned to take us. Ain't a better squirrel dog in the county than Old Bill. What did you name your dog?"

"I just calls him Blue. He already come to me when I calls him dat."

Except for the pork curing in the smoke house, which would be divided up later, the rest was split up, packed on ice, and folks departed with it. After eating my fill of pork chops that night, I went off to our room to go to bed while everyone else was still gnawing on the bones.

I kept my special things under the bed. Among them were two cigar boxes. One of them contained the beards from wild turkey gobblers my daddy had shot. The other one contained my arrowhead collection.

What I wanted to do was place the one my brother Ned had given me inside the box with the others.

When I reached under the bed for that box something rough scraped my arm. Bending down, I looked beneath the bed to see what foreign object had invaded the space.

It was a rope. Evidently a long one, because it was coiled up in a bundle, and when I felt of it, it felt damp as if it had been submerged in water.

CHAPTER SEVENTEEN

BACK TO SQUARE ONE

I didn't ever remember seeing that rope before. And what was it doing underneath the bed? My brother Fred had to have put it there, and I intended to ask him about it as soon as he came to bed.

All kinds of impossible thoughts were racing through my head as I snuggled underneath the quilts waiting for my brother to come to bed and give me some answers. Unfortunately, Ned was with him when he came in, and I knew I would have to wait until he went to sleep before I could whisper an inquiry to Fred.

They must have been exceedingly tired from the long, hard day at the hog killing, because they both went to sleep and began snoring in unison almost as soon as their heads hit the pillows. Now I would have to wait until tomorrow.

I must have been tired, too. I figured with all the questions floating around in my head I would toss and turn all night, but somewhere between a toss and a turn, I fell dead asleep.

The first thing to pop in my mind when I awoke the next morning was to see what Fred had to say about the rope. But when I sat up and looked around, the room was empty. I also noticed, while I slipped on my clothes, that it wasn't as cold as yesterday morning. There was no ice in the water bucket on the front porch. Fred had been correct; it was getting warmer.

After I washed up I rushed into the kitchen expecting to find my brothers, but no one was there except my momma. After a proper greeting to her, I inquired as to the whereabouts of Ned and Fred.

"They have gone to cut and haul more firewood with your Uncle Curvin," she answered.

"Again? We got plenty of wood."

"I believe they plan to sell a load or two today."

"So are they gonna be gone all day?"

"I expect so," she said as she slid a plate in front of me.

It had a fresh pork chop on it, fried up with a crusty, brown coating, along with a fresh fried egg, a biscuit, and syrup from the syrup-making. I ate it all up and thought about what a fortunate boy I was to receive such a fine meal. I told Momma how good it was, too.

"What you got on your mind today?" she asked.

"Uh—nothing, yet," I answered as I sopped my plate clean with the last remnant of my biscuit.

"Good, because I need for you to go to Miss Lena's Store to get me a box of salt and five pounds of sugar."

"You need me to go right now?"

"No, just sometime today."

Her request was welcome to my ears because I wanted

to go over to the store and see if I could hear any news. And I wanted to talk to Poudlum and get his observation about the rope under the bed. While I put my plate in the dishwater pan, I told my momma, "I'll go right away, but I may be gone awhile 'cause I want to go over to Poudlum's house."

"Why you want to go all the way over there?"

"He got a puppy for his birthday, a bluetick hound from over in Mississippi, that he's planning on making into a squirrel dog. I want to go see his new puppy, and I might take Old Bill with me just so he and the pup can get to know each other before they hunt together."

"All right, but don't you let Old Bill be fighting with no other dogs."

"I won't," I told her, knowing all the while there wasn't any dog hereabouts that wanted to get into a scrap with Old Bill. He was a black and tan hound. He was getting on up in years, and I could remember him as a puppy from back when I was in the first grade of school. Old Bill had a reputation as the best squirrel dog around, plus he was extremely smart for a dog, and would obey most anything I told him to do.

On one occasion I had seen him clamp down on a rattlesnake with his jaws and sling it around so hard that he popped that snake's head clean off, and there wasn't a critter in the woods he wouldn't take on, so it was a comfort to have him accompany me when I departed toward Miss Lena's Store.

I had to shed my jacket about halfway there, and I noticed Old Bill as he trotted along beside me had his black-marked tongue hanging out of the side of his mouth. Yep, it was definitely getting warmer. When we rounded the corner from Friendship Road onto Center Point Road, I was elated to see Poudlum sitting on the steps of Miss Lena's Store licking on a grape Popsicle, the same color as the spots on the puppy nestled between his legs.

When we got there Old Bill went over and lay down under the big oak tree next to the store. I nodded to Poudlum and he let Blue loose. We watched as Poudlum's new puppy trotted over and started sniffing around Old Bill's head. My dog ignored the puppy at first, but finally raised his head and licked Blue's little face, and we knew he had accepted the puppy.

"You think dem dogs can communicate wid each other?" Poudlum asked. "I don't mean talk like we does to each other, but maybe know what each other is thinking?"

I sat down next to Poudlum on the steps as we watched the two dogs and told him, "Yeah, I figure that. What do you think they would be saying to each other if they could talk?"

Poudlum observed for a few moments and said, "I think yo' dog is saying 'Hey, little dog, I likes you and think you might could be a good hunting dog,' dat's what I think."

"What you think your puppy is saying?"

"He saying, 'Hey, big dog, I wants to be a good hunter like you.' Yeah dat's what he saying."

Enough dog talk, I thought, and said, "I'm glad you came over this way, because if you hadn't, I was gonna walk over to your house and see if you heard anything about the money."

"Naw, I ain't heard nothing. Has you?"

I told him about the rope under our bed and he caught his breath, and said, "You think yo' brother Fred pulled dat money out of de creek?"

"That's what I was thinking. Where else would a wet rope come from? But I haven't had a chance to ask him about it. I'm gonna get me a Popsicle, you want another one?"

I went into the store and got us both a lime Popsicle and we went over and sat down under the big oak tree with the two dogs. In between licks, Poudlum said, "It looks like besides being rich, yo' brother wuz right about the weather. It's getting a lot warmer."

"If he found that money, I think he'll share it with us. Let's just meet right here after church tomorrow and go fishing with him and see what he's got to show us."

"You think he gonna show us de money?"

"Well, he did say he had a surprise for us. What else could it be?"

My brothers didn't get home until long after dark that night and I barely remembered them coming into our room and getting into bed. The next morning we all had to get up and get all spruced up for church, so I still never had an opportunity to be alone with Fred. Finally, I resolved to say nothing to him and just wait and let him tell us about the money.

As soon as Sunday dinner was over Fred and I lit out to meet Poudlum. On the way we stopped at our hideout and collected the food we had hidden up in the rafters of the cotton house.

Poudlum was right on time, and the three of us began

walking toward the creek, bathed in warm sunshine, once again headed for the Cypress Hole.

After we set up camp and stacked up some firewood, Fred said, "Y'all remember I told you I had a surprise for you?"

Poudlum nudged me and whispered out of the side of his mouth, "Here it come."

Fred reached into his pack, and with his arm submerged deep within it, he said, "It's just three days until Christmas so this is kind of like birthday and Christmas presents for y'all."

Poudlum and I grinned at each other because we knew he was going to pull out big rolls of money, so when he pulled out two books, we were both dumbfounded, stunned, and moved to complete silence.

"They are both a little bit worn," he said. "But they still in pretty fair condition. I bought them at the library in Grove Hill yesterday. I heard a while back they were having a used book sale so I got Uncle Curvin to stop by it on our way to deliver a load of wood. I used some of the money I earned selling firewood to buy them for y'all."

We sat like two people made of stone as he handed a book to each of us. "I've read both of them," he told us. "Y'all are going to really like them. *The Adventures of Tom Sawyer* is for you," he said to me.

"And that's *The Adventures of Huckleberry Finn* for you, Poudlum. Both them books reminded me of y'all, especially the one about Huckleberry Finn. He helps his friend Jim escape down the Mississippi River like y'all helped Jake escape across the Tombigbee River. When you finish reading each one you can trade with each other. What y'all think?" he said as he sat back and observed us.

I looked at Poudlum and Poudlum looked at me. We didn't know what to say or think.

"What's the matter?" Fred asked. They were both written by Mr. Mark Twain and take place over on the Mississippi River. I thought y'all would really like those two books."

I could see the disappointment and the hurt in his eyes, so I said, "The books are great. Thank you very much."

"Something's wrong, though. I can tell it. What is it?"

"It's just that we thought you were going to give us something besides a book."

"What?"

Poudlum couldn't stand it any longer. "Ain't you got de money?" he blurted out.

"Huh?" my brother said with a bewildered look on his face.

"Where's the money?" I demanded.

"What money you talking about?"

I still wasn't sure my brother wasn't messing with us, so I said, "Why the money the bank robbers stole and hid in the creek, of course."

"Why in the world would y'all come to the conclusion I had that money?"

"Because of the rope," I said.

"Huh?"

"They's a big coil of wet rope under our bed. Now don't you try and tell me it wasn't the rope attached to the bag of money hidden in the Cypress Hole by Jesse and Frank, the bank robbers."

"I-I found that rope!" my brother stuttered.

"Where?" I demanded.

"I found it beside the road on Center Point Road close to Miss Lena's Store. I figure it fell off somebody's truck, and it was a perfectly good rope so I brought it home and stuck it under the bed."

I could tell by my brother's voice he was telling the truth. A glance at Poudlum and I could tell he thought the same.

"Y'all both know I wouldn't lie to you about something like that," my brother told us. "I might fib to you about something not real important, and kid with you, but what I told you is the truth."

I looped my arm up around his broad shoulders on one side and Poudlum did the same on the other side. "We believe you," I told him. "It's just that now we're back to square one."

"Yeah, we knows dat, Fred," Poudlum said. "It was mighty kind and thoughtful of you to get dem books for us to read."

"Let's just get us a fire going, do some fishing, and forget about that," I told them both.

The creek was flowing softly and the fish were biting hard. We had forgotten about bank robbers and everything outside of our small world. Fred was cleaning the fish while Poudlum and I caught them. Darkness was almost upon us when we pulled in our poles and gathered around the fire, ready to drop our fish into the hot, sizzling grease. That's when the ruckus started.

At first we thought it was a bear or something crashing

through the woods, but then we saw the headlights through the woods. It was a vehicle rumbling down the trail through the woods toward the Cypress Hole.

Poudlum's eyes grew large, I gasped, and Fred stood up and said, "What in the heck is going on?"

A moment later we were bathed in the headlights of a car and a rough voice called out, "You boys just hold it right there where you are!"

I recognized the voice. It was Sheriff Crowe. "Don't y'all try running now, you hear?" he called out.

Poudlum and I cringed, but my brother wasn't easily intimidated. "We got no reason to run anywhere. What you want with us, sheriff?"

The sheriff ignored Fred as another car came flying up behind his and two of his deputies piled out. They all walked up close next to our fire and they were mighty imposing with their big pistols on their hips and their shiny badges on their chests.

The sheriff spit tobacco juice on our fire, and while it was sizzling, he said, "What you boys up to?"

Still unfazed, Fred responded, "We were fixing to fry us up some fish when y'all came busting in here. What can we do for you, sheriff?"

"You hush up, boy," Sheriff Crowe said. "I'll ask the questions. You sit down there on the ground with your little brother and y'all's little nigger friend."

Reluctantly, Fred sank down protectively next to Poudlum and me.

The sheriff hitched his pants up over his ample belly, spat into the fire again, and said, "I didn't come way out here to waste my time. I'm looking for some information and I expect y'all to give it to me."

Still not intimidated, my brash brother said, "We have already asked you what you wanted."

"Boy," the sheriff said as he stared hard through his beady eyes at Fred, "I don't like your attitude. You keep up with that mouth of yours and I might have one of my deputies dip you in the creek."

I nudged Fred and whispered out of the corner of my mouth, "Don't say nothing else!"

The sheriff's deputies had spread out around us by now and we all knew there was no escape from them.

The dusk had faded to dark and flames from our fire licked up and cast shimmering shadows all around while the sheriff said, "Like I told y'all, it's way past my supper time, and I don't intend to tarry here long. Now which one of y'all wants to tell me where the money is?"

I finally found my voice and said, "If you're talking about the money the bank robbers took, then none of us have it nor know where it is. Talk is that it washed on down the creek, or the robbers hid it somewhere else and told you a big fat lie, sheriff."

He acted like he hadn't heard a word I said, leaned over toward Poudlum and said, "How about you, little nigger, you know where that money is?"

"Naw, naw, sir, I ain't got no idea where dat money is."

One of the sheriff's deputies piped up and said, "Let me dip 'em in the creek, sheriff. I bet they'll talk then."

My brother took exception to that threat and stood up. Fred was almost fifteen years old, six feet and three inches tall, and solid muscle. I had no doubts he could whip any one of those three fat officers of the law, but they had guns and they were the law. I tugged on his britches leg, and when he looked down I said, "Uh-uh, don't."

"Put 'em in the car," the sheriff instructed his deputies. "We'll see what they have to say from a jail cell. Watch that big'un."

CHAPTER EIGHTEEN

INCARCERATED

I was scared and I knew Poudlum was too. He sat in the middle between Fred and me in the back seat of the car. I knew he hadn't lost his sense of humor when he said, "Seems like we can't never finish no fishing trip. Either outlaws or de legal law keep messing dem up."

They had put us in the back seat of the deputies' car and the sheriff led the way in his. They weren't saying anything in the front and we got real quiet, too. There were no inside door handles and we were locked inside the car. It had gotten real dark outside, but I knew we were still on Center Point Road from the sound of the car's tires on the dirt road.

The vehicle came to a stop, accelerated, and then a smooth whining sound came up from the road, which told me we were on Highway 84 heading toward Grove Hill.

"What y'all think dey gonna do wid us?" Poudlum whispered.

"Don't be scared," Fred whispered back. "They're most likely just going to try to scare us 'cause they think we might know something about where the money is. When we don't show up home tomorrow our folks will come looking for us."

When the deputies' car slowed down and made some turns, I knew we were in Grove Hill. "You all right, Poudlum?" I asked him.

"Naw, and if I can just get out of dis police car, den I'll never complain about going to church again."

"Me neither," I told him. "In fact, if we get out of this mess I'll go to your church with you."

"Hey," Fred spoke up quickly while the deputies were out of the car and preparing to open our doors. "Don't let 'em make you say anything that is not so! They'll probably separate us and ask a lot of questions. Just pretend it's a bad dream and it'll be over soon."

My brother was correct, they did separate us. They took me into a room with no windows and left me locked up in there by myself for what seemed like forever. It just had a little table with cigarette burns all along the edge of it and two cold metal chairs.

I was sitting in one of them shivering from the cold and from fear when the sheriff came in and closed the door behind him. He pulled out the other chair, breathed a heavy sigh and deposited his huge bulk into it. He didn't say anything while he took a Camel cigarette out of the packet and tapped the end of it on the table before he put it into his mouth.

He pulled out a Zippo lighter from his pocket, flipped the lid up with his thumb, and twirled the tiny wheel against the flint causing it to explode into a small flame, which he put to the end of his Camel and began to inhale deeply. The smoke twirled around and about his face and floated in the air between us. I was scared real bad, but tried to remember the words of wisdom my brother had given before they separated us. I decided to concentrate on them and do like he said, just pretend it was a bad dream. I also wished my daddy was home right then.

"You remember where that money is yet, boy," the sheriff said as he took a long drag on his Camel.

I didn't say anything. I didn't know what to say. I was just trying to still my trembling knees beneath the table.

"We know you boys found that money. We heard y'all been traipsing all up and down that creek. Now if you'll just tell us where it is, we'll take you home and you can sleep in your own bed. Otherwise, you gonna be sleeping in one of my jail cells tonight."

"I don't know where no money is, sheriff. We looked for it just like a lot of folks did, but we didn't find it," I told him in a trembling voice.

"Listen, boy," he spat out at me. "I done talked to them two bank robbers and they both say you boys probably got the money. Now you tell me what y'all done gone and done with it!"

Being accused of doing something wrong that you know you didn't do is a bad thing, but being accused by a person in authority is even worse, especially when they make it evident they think you are a liar.

I told the sheriff repeatedly that I had no idea where the money was, and he finally stormed out of the room, and I heard him out in the hallway as he gave instructions to his staff. "I want y'all to lock 'em up. Put them in separate cells."

It was about the worst thing that had ever happened to me in my life when a jailer led me down a dim hallway with steel doors with little narrow slots in them to my left and right. He stopped in front of one of them, inserted his key and swung it open. Numbly, I followed his slight push and walked into the steel cage and heard the metallic clicking as the door slammed shut behind me.

It was dark inside the cell with the only light coming from the moonlight through a barred window up high on the wall. Looking down, I could see the dark outlines of a narrow bed. I reached down and touched the rough blanket on it and marveled at the contrast between it and the soft, smooth quilt on my bed at home.

I felt the cold sinking into my bones, but I refused to get under that alien blanket. I just lay down on top of it and curled up into a ball, tucking my cold hands between my thighs.

To go to sleep I used the memory Poudlum had taught me during the misery of the cotton field of how to take your mind to a finer place while your body suffered. I concentrated on imagining I was safe at home, warm and secure under my momma's quilt, and soon I found a peaceful sleep, even though my body was incarcerated in a miserable place.

I thought I was having another bad dream, but quickly realized it was morning when I heard the metallic click in the door to my cell. When I looked up I could see the light from the morning sun sifting through the bars of the window up above.

The door swung open and I heard a beautiful sound. It was the voice of my Uncle Curvin. "Son," he said as he entered and stood over my bed, "are you all right?"

They took us to a large room, and I was overjoyed to see Fred and Poudlum. What really surprised me was that Mister Alfred Jackson, the lawyer, was there too. He was in a heated argument with the sheriff.

"You have overstepped the boundaries of your authority, sir, by locking up these young boys!"

"I'm the law in this county!" the sheriff countered.

"I doubt you'll be come next election," Mr. Jackson almost shouted. "Now, I demand their release, or I'll initiate legal action against you!"

Sheriff Crowe sputtered and puffed out his chest, but in the end he relented and said, "You take 'em and get out of my jail."

We were all too happy to accommodate him, and Uncle Curvin took us all over to Mr. Jackson's office, up a long set of steps that led to the floor up on top of the First Bank of Grove Hill, where we all gathered around a big conference table.

Uncle Curvin began by saying, "I know y'all are all hungry and want to go home, but they's something Mr. Jackson and I have to tell y'all first."

I was so hungry I could have eaten that table with a little blackberry jam on it. We had missed our supper and had no breakfast, but I was willing to listen.

Mr. Jackson walked into the room with a big sack in his hands. He didn't say anything, just turned the sack upside down and big bundles of money came tumbling out of it onto the table. "Behold," he said. "Here's the money the bank robbers stole."

We all just sat there, bug-eyed, wondering what was going on.

Mr. Jackson began to explain. "Mr. Curvin, a witness to the bank robbery, found the money, boys. But it was your efforts that enabled him to do so. I'll let him tell you how it happened."

We sat there, stunned, but Uncle Curvin didn't make us wait long.

"You boys remember that night of the sleet storm when we all took refuge in the hidey hole? I had to get up some-time after midnight to relieve myself and it had stopped sleeting and cleared off. There was a bright moon and I could see so good I decided to take one more look around the Cypress Hole. I been fishing that hole since before you boys got born, and I can cross those shoals above the deep water blindfolded, even if I am a little bit crippled.

"After I crossed over the creek that night I found that mark on the black gum tree with my flashlight, the one y'all told me about later, then I found the rope and pulled that sack of money out of the water. I brought it back to the hidey hole and was sleeping on top of it when y'all left that morning. After I found out the sheriff had hauled y'all in I took it to Mr. Jackson, and then we came and got y'all out of jail.

"Sheriff Crowe and his passel of deputies had been keeping a keen eye on me ever since he seen me bring you boys to the trial with me. I suppose he figured we were in cahoots. So I just left the money in the hidey hole until I found out the sheriff had taken y'all, because I knew if him or any one of his deputies caught me with the money, then it wouldn't never got back to the rightful owners. I didn't dare tell anyone, including you boys, that I had the money for fear the sheriff would find out."

Mr. Jackson began to rake the money back into the sack, and said, "Mr. Curvin has insisted that you three boys get credit for the recovery of the money and receive the five hundred dollar reward. I will notify the bank of the recovery of their funds, and I'll also notify the newspaper. I feel sure they will want to do a Christmas story on you boys.

"Christmas day is Wednesday, day after tomorrow. I know you boys want to go home and get some food and rest, but I'll be needing y'all back right here tomorrow so you can officially turn the money over to the bank while the paper takes a picture and interviews the three of you. Curvin, can you get the boys back here tomorrow about noon so we can put this incident behind us? It would be a good Christmas present for the community and everyone concerned."

"Yes, sir, Mr. Jackson," my uncle said. "I'll get them home, get them fed and rested, and talk to their folks and make sure they're here."

"Fine," Mr. Jackson said as he stood up and shook hands with each of us. He continued, "Now, boys, I know last night was a traumatic experience for you, but take it as a lesson that life isn't always fair. However, as you are experiencing now, truth and justice always prevails in the end."

It was a joyful ride home.

"You think dey really gon put us in de newspaper, Mister Curvin," Poudlum asked.

"I sure do," Uncle Curvin replied. "That's what Mr. Jackson said, and I'll put my money on him anytime."

Fred interjected, "Yeah, and everybody is going to know we spent the night in jail. They'll be calling us jailbirds, but we'll be rich jailbirds."

Just before we dropped Poudlum off at his house he tugged on my shirt sleeve and said, "You 'member what you said?"

"Huh?"

"You said if we got out of de mess we wuz in you would go to church wid me."

"Yeah, I said that," I answered.

"Well?" he asked as he got out of the truck and stood there in the road leading down to his house.

"I said it and I'll do it. This Sunday after Christmas I'll go to your church with you."

I could see him grinning there in the road as we pulled away.

My momma had a fine meal fixed for us when we got home. Uncle Curvin stayed and ate with us while he filled her and Ned in on all the details of the past two days. "I drove over to the Cypress Hole about dark yesterday to see if the boys were catching any fish. Sheriff Crowe and two of his deputies were hauling y'all off just when I got there. So I went on up to Grove Hill and found out they had 'em locked up. I stayed up there, slept all night in my truck, and the first thing this morning I went to see Mr. Jackson. I had the money with me, took it out of y'all's hidey hole on the way, and y'all know the rest of the story from there."

My momma was horrified when she heard the story. "Lord have mercy!" she said. "And all the time I thought they was over on the creek fishing all night instead of being locked up in the jail house by that sorry sheriff. I'll guarantee he won't ever be elected again. The colored folks will all be against him too because he put Poudlum in jail with y'all."

"Colored folks can't vote, Momma," Fred said.

"No, they can't," she said. But they can sure tell white voters what they think."

I couldn't believe the crowd of folks in front of the bank the next morning when we arrived in Grove Hill. After everybody had gathered around, Mr. Jackson called Fred, Poudlum, and me up next to him in front of the bank while some gentleman with the newspaper snapped photos of us.

Then Mr. Jackson hushed everyone and proceeded to tell the crowd we were heroes, and rightly so, had earned the five hundred dollar reward to be split between us. He went on to say the money would be invested in our names, and by the time we got ready to go to college there would be plenty of money to pay for it.

I heard him say all the money from the robbery had been recovered except for forty dollars, which he surmised the robbers had probably spent in their efforts to escape.

I saw Poudlum cut his eyes toward me, but I kept staring straight ahead because I figured two perfectly good pocket knives and two ruined fishing trips were worth at least that amount.

The festive atmosphere of the occasion slowly faded

and people dispersed to go about their business. Even Mr. Jackson finally excused himself when he said to all of us, "Merry Christmas, boys, and let this be still another lesson for y'all—out of everything bad something good always comes."

After he was gone, Poudlum asked Uncle Curvin, "Mister Curvin, what you 'spect Mr. Jackson meant by dat?"

My uncle thought for a few moments before he responded. When he did, I knew he was right. "What I think, boys, is that the bank robbery was bad, but the fact that y'all can all now go to college is good."

Poudlum tilted his head back for a moment before he said, "Uh-huh, I 'spect you right about dat, Mister Curvin."

After mine and Poudlum's mommas emerged from the Piggly-Wiggly laden with oranges and nuts for Christmas, we all loaded up and headed back toward home.

My brother Ned had cut us a Christmas tree and we watched that night as Momma placed some teacakes under it for Santa Claus. I noticed she had a smile on her face like she knew something we didn't when she shooed us all off to bed.

The next morning, Christmas Day, I realized she had known something we didn't after a pair of strong, familiar arms pulled me out of bed, and I received the best possible Christmas present in the world. From all the way across the great Pacific Ocean, and across the continental United States, my daddy had come all the way home to Alabama for Christmas.

Chapter Nineteen

BLACK ANGELS

had never seen a coconut before. It was the largest nut
I could ever have imagined, and I quickly found out it
was a different kind of nut. It was almost as difficult to
crack as a black walnut, but it had delectable juice inside it
surrounded by an abundance of sweet meat. It taught me
there were many great wonders in the world just waiting
for me to discover them.

But my father had brought us something much more
important than coconuts. He had brought us opportunity
and hope for a better life through his sacrifices and hard
work. He had saved a great deal of money and I knew our
lives were about to change.

Immediately after Christmas we began packing things
into the new pickup truck he had driven home. Soon we
would be on our way to a new home and my daddy on to
his new job with the State of Alabama.

But first I had a promise to keep. On the Sunday following Christmas Momma starched and ironed my white shirt
and I left early walking over to Poudlum's house.

Poudlum and his brothers and sisters were all loading onto the back of his daddy's ancient pickup truck when I arrived. As we rode along, I thought what a stark contrast I must have made, riding along Center Point Road towards Coffeeville with my white face among the dark ones.

I had seen the outside of the church before when Uncle Curvin and I had picked up Poudlum there, but I had never seen the inside.

Poudlum escorted me in with his arm draped over my shoulder while colored folks nodded greetings on each side of the aisle, some of them saying, "Hey, Mister Ted."

"Tell 'em to quit calling me that, Poudlum," I whispered to him.

"But dat's who you is," he whispered back.

I resigned myself to it and slid into a pew with Poudlum. It was as hard as the ones in my church.

I heard the doors close and it got real quiet inside that church. It was hot, too, and they had fans like we did, squares of hard cardboard with pictures of Jesus on them, stapled to oversized Popsicle sticks. As I cut my eyes around I could see colored faces fanning all around me.

We didn't have a choir at my church, but they did at Poudlum's. They came silently marching in, wearing black robes and hats with lots of flowers in them, and seated themselves in a row of chairs to the left of the pulpit.

There was no piano or organ; they just began a melodious humming until everyone was completely settled. And then, on some unrecognizable sign, they broke into a song about Jesus, love, salvation, and absolution. The tiny hairs on my arms and neck literally stood on end while they sang "Deep River" and "Steal Away." They sang like angels, beautiful and haunting like nothing I had ever heard before, like something not from this world.

The choir kind of wound down and the preacher took the pulpit. He was a large man, and with a voice to match as it boomed across the congregation and reverberated off the walls when he said, "Praise de Lawd, we fixing to have church here today. If de devil be anywhere close by, he needs to tuck his forked tail twixt his legs and hightail it on out of here, 'cause Jesus is wid us!"

"Amen, brother!" someone shouted from the back of the congregation. I was shocked when people from all over the congregation began talking back to the preacher. In my church everyone sat quiet and didn't utter a sound, but not here.

"Praise Jesus!" someone called out across the aisle, and up in front of me, a lady with a hat as big as a cotton basket cried out, "Amen, tell it brother!"

It was that way throughout the entire service. Folks would get carried away and participate in the sermon from right out in the church. And that big preacher didn't seem to mind; in fact, I believe he encouraged their participation.

But he still dominated the service. He held his large hands up in a signal for silence and said, "Before we gets into de sermon, I want to recognize our visitors."

He recognized some folks from over in Georgia who were visiting their family. Next he pointed out some children from down in Mobile who had come up to visit with their grandparents.

Then, to my horror, he said, "And we got us a special

visitor wid us today. He a friend of the Robinsons, and from what I understand is a friend of all us colored folks."

He chuckled, and said, "Just look around, he won't be hard to find. He's over on de third row next to young Mister Poudlum. Let's everybody make Mister Ted welcome!"

Black hands reached out to touch me, pat me on the shoulder, stroke my blond hair, and those who couldn't reach me called out to me. I was greatly relieved when the preacher said, "And now, the sisters in the choir are going to treat us to their rendition of that old spiritual 'Go Tell It on the Mountain.' Everybody join in."

Go, tell it on the mountain,
Over the hills and everywhere
Go, tell it on the mountain,
That Jesus Christ is born

While shepherds kept their watching
Over silent flocks by night
Behold throughout the heavens
There shone a holy light

After the beautiful sound of the song faded away the preacher began preaching, and he preached long and hard. Hunger, thirst, and all physical things departed from my mind. It felt like it had in the cotton field when Poudlum had taught me how to endure the hardship of picking cotton by separating your mind from your body, except in this case you didn't have to put forth any effort because the preacher did it for you.

He started out speaking gentle and low, talking about suffering, and how none of us had endured anything near to the extent our Savior had. He said how we all spent eternity depended on how we spent our mortal days on earth, and that someday we all would rid ourselves of our mortal bond and set off toward eternity.

It wasn't too far into his sermon before his voice grew and he picked up a rhythm. And about that time the amens and praises increased as the congregation began to sway in rhythm with the preacher's voice. Pretty soon folks were talking back to the preacher after almost every sentence he uttered. They were caught up in something special as they called out, "Sweet Jesus," "Yes, Lawd," and "Amen, brother!"

His voice grew in volume and intensity, and I began to feel something myself and wanted to shout it out. I just didn't know what. What I did know was that that church was rocking with folks shouting, jumping, and clapping their hands.

The preacher wound the congregation down with just as much expertise as he had wound them up. His voice receded in volume, turned into almost a whisper as the shouts evolved into tears. Finally, the choir of black angels sang a moving rendition of "Sometimes I Feel Like a Motherless Child," and then it was over.

I got to see Poudlum one more time before school started back. It was when Uncle Curvin took us up there to get us an official copy of the papers where Mr. Jackson had invested our reward money.

After that, while my uncle was taking care of some other

business, Poudlum, Fred and I walked over to the drug store. When we walked in, I saw the man who had thrown Poudlum and me out of the store back in the summer when I had attempted to have ice cream at the counter with him.

At first, I was afraid he was going to do the same thing again, but he surprised me. While we observed, he bent over behind the counter and emerged with three cones of chocolate ice cream, which he handed over to us and said, "Boys, these cones are on the house. You young fellows enjoy them."

We thanked him, and then bought us some comic books and some hard candy before we walked back outside, licking our cones.

While we were rolling up our comic books and tucking them in our pockets, Poudlum said, "Dat sho wuz nice of dat gentleman to give us dese ice cream cones. You think he would let us sit down at de counter and have us a dish of ice cream like we tried to dat one time before?"

"No, not yet," I told him. "But one day, one day soon."

∽

ABOUT THE AUTHOR

Ted M. Dunagan was born in 1943 in rural southwestern Alabama. He attended Georgia State University, and served for three years in the Army as a member of the 101st Airborne Division and Special Forces Training Group. Dunagan is now retired after a career in the cosmetics and fragrance industry. He writes features and columns for the *Monticello News* in Monticello, Georgia, where he lives with his wife. Dunagan was named Georgia Author of the Year 2009 in the Young Adult category for his debut novel *A Yellow Watermelon*.

READ MORE ADVENTURES OF
TED AND POUDLUM IN

a Yellow
WATERMELON

by TED M. DUNAGAN

"In *A Yellow Watermelon*, Ted refuses to be an observer of life in rural Alabama of 1948. He's in the middle of the action, looking and listening and thinking. He learns secrets and stirs up dangers that force him to take a courageous stand against long established customs that are unfair and dishonest. What can an 'almost twelve year old' do to make a difference? With the help of forbidden friends, Ted's inventive solutions will surprise the reader and keep the pages turning to the tasty end of the story."
— AILEEN KILGORE HENDERSON

"A fine, well-told tale of friendship between two smart, likable boys—one white, one black. Memorable [and] generous-hearted."
— *Kirkus Reviews*

ISBN 978-1-58838-197-2
240 pages • $21.95

Available from your favorite bookstore or online at
WWW.NEWSOUTHBOOKS.COM/WATERMELON

More titles from Junebug Books

LONGLEAF
ROGER REID

Jason and his forest-smart friend Leah must survive
a harrowing night lost in Alabama's Conecuh National Forest.

JB

SPACE
ROGER REID

Jason returns to help a group of scientists
solve a mystery near NASA's Marshall Space Flight Center.

JB

CRACKER'S MULE
BILLY MOORE

A boy spending a summer in 1950s Alabama
suffers ridicule as he raises a blind mule.

JB

LITTLE BROTHER REAL SNAKE
BILLY MOORE

The son of a brave Plains warrior overcomes challenges
on a quest to take his place in his tribe.

JB

THE GOLD DISC OF COOSA
VIRGINIA POUNDS BROWN

A exciting account of the historic meeting between the
explorer DeSoto and the last of the Alabama Moundbuilders.

Read chapters, purchase books, and learn more at
WWW.NEWSOUTHBOOKS.COM/JUNEBUG